D0005101

ALSO BY KATE BANKS

Dillon Dillon
Howie Bowles and Uncle Sam
Howie Bowles, Secret Agent

PICTURE BOOKS

Mama's Coming Home
Close Your Eyes
The Turtle and the Hippopotamus
A Gift from the Sea
The Night Worker
The Bird, the Monkey, and the Snake in the Jungle
And If the Moon Could Talk
Baboon
Spider Spider

WALK SOFTLY, RACHEL

KATE BANKS
WALK SOFTLY, RACHEL

Frances Foster Books
Farrar, Straus and Giroux
New York

Copyright © 2003 by Kate Banks
All rights reserved
Distributed in Canada by Douglas and McIntyre Ltd.
Printed in the United States of America
Designed by Jennifer Crilly
First edition, 2003
1 3 5 7 9 10 8 6 4 2

Library of Congress Cataloging-in-Publication Data
Banks, Kate, date.
  Walk softly, Rachel / Kate Banks.— 1st ed.
    p. cm.
  Summary: When fourteen-year-old Rachel reads the journal of her brother,
who died when she was seven, she learns secrets that help her understand her
parents and herself.
  ISBN 0-374-38230-1
  [1. Family problems—Fiction.   2. Emotional problems—Fiction.
3. Death—Fiction.   4. Secrets—Fiction.   5. Journals—Fiction.]   I. Title.

PZ7.B22594 Wal 2003
[Fic]—dc21

                                                                    2002026503

FOR MY SISTER AMY

WALK SOFTLY, RACHEL

ONE

On a table in the living room is a photograph of three women joined together in a pattern of overlapping shoulders, arms, and legs. I am the one in the middle. That's my mother on the left. My grandmother is on the right. We are all called Rachel. Rachels one, two, and three. I'm Rachel three. My father is not in the picture. He says it's because his name is not Rachel. But he's not telling the truth, not the whole truth anyway. He does not like to look at himself in photographs. Nor does he like to look at himself in mirrors. Or in storefront windows. There is something he does not want to see. I once had a brother. He is not in the picture either. He died when I was seven. Now I am fourteen. His name was Jake. In a way, this story is about Jake. But mostly it's just about people.

TWO

It's spring, my favorite time of the year. The air is cool but sweet with the smell of mud, fresh grass, and new leaves. It's nighttime, and I hear the wail of neighborhood tomcats. I can see their dark shadows sweeping like spirits through the streets. I am walking home from a party. A going-away party. My best friend, Adrian Hess, is leaving town. He and his family are moving to a remote part of Africa where a letter takes months, years, even a lifetime to arrive. If it ever does. There are no telephones. None that work, anyway. My connection to Adrian has been bluntly severed and my body throbs with a dull ache. I have stuffed myself with potato chips and cake to fill the longing that's spreading inside of me like an acid stain. I wrap my arms around myself, trying to hang on to the feeling of Adrian's last hug. In my head Jim Morrison bangs out the final refrain of "Love Her Madly." Then the music stops short just as it does in a game of musical chairs. I am left without a seat. And I am sad. The sadness travels through my body and reawakens old griefs. Other hurts, long since forgotten, that have settled cozily into my bones and become a part of who I am.

I walk faster, trying to outpace my feelings. My mind races ahead, trying to outrun my thoughts. I shift my attention from one object to another etched against the sable sky. A church steeple, a weather vane, a row of chimneyed rooftops. On the hill off to the left is the old mill. Its solid frame structure glows in the moonlight like a skeleton from the past. This village, where I live, used to be a mill town. A town of flour and bread. A town of humble bakers. Most of the people living here are their descendants. I am one of them. My great-grandparents were millers. They had a bakery at the bottom of this very road. But times have changed. People no longer depend on milling for their livelihood. Still, they have not forgotten. Bread and baking are drafted in the blueprint of the town, cataloged in our DNA.

Each year there is a bread festival, both a reminder and a celebration of the past. It is coming up in just a few weeks. Shops will close for the day and people will head for the streets with homemade loaves of piping-hot bread. Every kind imaginable. There will be music, food, and games. At sunset an award will be presented to the maker of the tastiest loaf. Then we will feast on bread and fill ourselves with our past. For days after, the air will smoke with particles of flour and vibrate with the pungent smell of ripe yeast. In a final gesture, the graduating high school students will gather in the streets to commemorate the bread strikes of the late 1800s, when workers pressed for higher pay and shorter hours. They will disguise themselves as bakers, coat themselves in flour, and march through town in one last act of rebellion before moving on. Then the dust will settle and life will return to normal. But the past will not be forgotten. Perhaps it never is.

Suddenly I feel a warm sensation travel through my body, from the tips of my toes to the roots of my hair. Tears well in my eyes. I feel like crying. Then a terrible thing happens. Something snaps in my body. A fuse blows. And I start to laugh. It is not the first time this has occurred. It happens a lot. I laugh when I want to cry. And I cry when I should be laughing. It's as if I have a short circuit somewhere. The saddest story in the world will send me into fits of laughter. The other day I passed a construction site just as a workman was hit on the head with a two-by-four. He started to bleed and I started to laugh. I couldn't help myself. He turned to me and said, "Hey, buddy, you ought to be a comedian."

The truth is I would love to be a comedian. To stand up on a stage, face an audience, and make them laugh. To rattle their funny bones and tickle their toes. To make them fall out of their seats and roll on the floor with laughter. To laugh until they cry. The trouble is I would be crying, too, because of this "thing." I call it the "thing" because it does not have a name. My parents have taken me to half a dozen therapists, but nothing helps. So here I am. My best friend in the world is leaving town and I am laughing. I'm glad it's dark and no one can see me. I hope no one can hear me. But I feel my voice traveling up the hill to the old mill, and I am afraid that the past is listening.

I reach out and touch an iron lamppost. Its cold, flat metal feels like a slap against my skin. I am nearly home. My house is at the end of the street. It is white, with green shutters, and it sits back from the road like a shadow box lit up among neatly pruned trees. The shrubs, carefully groomed, seem almost afraid to breathe in the quiet night air. The window at the top left is my bedroom. That one at the top right was Jake's. Or maybe I should say *is* Jake's. My mother left everything just as it was the day he died. The bed is still made. The shelves are lined with his books and sports trophies. My mother goes there sometimes and stands in the middle of the room. It's as though she's waiting for Jake to return. I used to go there, too, after Jake died. The sun would splash in on the wooden floor, and I could feel the warmth of life moving in circles around my feet. But I have not been back for a long time.

As strange as it may seem, I don't know very much about Jake. He was killed in a car accident when I was just seven years old. My parents don't talk about him and I'm too embarrassed to ask. But I remember his straight blond hair and green eyes, his laugh, the graceful way he moved when he ran. He was a runner, always competing and always winning. I remember the feeling of having a big brother who played hide-and-seek with me, who carried me to school on his broad shoulders, who opened presents with me on birthdays and holidays. I remember the night Jake died. Dr. Moser at the front door bearing the news like a sickly burden. The grief that spread over the house, trickling into its foundations. I remember my mother's tears and my father's anguish, my grandmother's hugs. Then I remember waiting. Waiting for Jake to walk through the front door and into the kitchen. Finally I remember realizing, knowing, that Jake would never return. Then I remember forgetting. There is a hole. No memory for six months, maybe a year, maybe two. Then I recall stepping into another life. I am no longer the little one, no longer a sister. I have become Rachel, an only child. My mother, Rachel two, has gone back to work, and Rachel one, my grandmother, is there when I get home from school.

I know there are memories I have lost. They have been erased from my being. Others are still there, sleeping soundly, somewhere inside of me.

My eyes are drawn to Jake's bedroom window. It is pitch black. Tonight the blackness pulls at me like a horseshoe magnet. As I look at that window, something in me stirs. Tonight I am curious about that room. I am curious about Jake. Tonight I wish he were here, alive.

I open the front door. My parents are still up in the living room. They are both dressed normally now. But it is hard to forget that my father passes his days clothed in white, like an angel or a savior. He is the chief surgeon at Peat Memorial Hospital. My mother spends her days draped in black. She is a circuit judge. It is hard to forget that they hold the fate of other lives in their hands.

Rachel two, my mother, is sewing a button on one of Dad's shirts. He's forever losing buttons. Dad looks up from a medical journal and smiles. "Hi, sweet pea," he says. He's called me "sweet pea" since the day I was born. He tugs at my hair. I bend down and he tries to kiss me on the cheek right where Adrian has kissed me.

"Not there," I say, pulling back.

"Beg your pardon," Dad says. Then he takes my hand and pecks it gallantly.

Mom puts down her sewing. "Did Adrian have a nice send-off?" she asks.

"I guess so," I say, flopping onto the couch. I cannot hide my sadness. I don't even bother to try.

"Friends come and go, Rachel," Mom says matter-of-factly. "That's part of life."

"Are we going to have to put you on a life-support system to get you through this?" Dad jokes. He jokes a lot, especially about serious things.

"Could be," I answer.

"Where did you get that sweatshirt?" asks Rachel two. She is trying not to focus on my insides, which makes her uncomfortable.

"I got it from Adrian," I say. I look down at the stained and oversized bundle I am wearing and I smile. Every time I put it on, I will think of Adrian. I will feel his arms in the sleeves. It's hard to believe that the only tangible thing I am left with is this length of cloth and the body cells Adrian's sloughed off on its surface.

"It looks like it needs a good washing," says Rachel two.

"Please don't wash it," I say.

Rachel two laughs nervously. "There will be other Adrians," she says. I know what she means, but I don't want to hear it. I don't want to be reminded that the bubble I call Adrian will eventually pop or lose all of its air. And that there will be room for someone else.

"Priscilla Moser was asking about you just the other day," Mom says. "Why don't you two get together?" Priscilla is the daughter of Paul and Betty Moser, my parents' best friends.

I shrug, unmoved. I don't want to sound mean, but I can't help myself. "Priscilla takes up too much space," I say.

Dad makes another joke. "How can that be?" he asks. "She must weigh all of eighty-five pounds."

I nod absently. "You want to know the truth?" I say. I don't wait for an answer. "I don't like Priscilla. And she doesn't like me." I look down at Mom's sewing. "You can't replace friends like buttons on shirts," I say.

Rachel two nods and judiciously bows out of the conversation.

"How about a game of chess before turning in?" Dad asks. "I've got the board all set up."

I go over to the card table and sit down. Rachel two has moved to the kitchen. I hear her in the background clattering around, opening drawers, banging cupboards shut.

I am distracted and don't play well.

"Check," says Dad. I lose. I am tired.

"Good night, everyone," I say. I go upstairs to bed. I don't bother to brush my teeth. I don't wash my face. I don't take off Adrian's sweatshirt. Before falling asleep, I look around my room. At my volleyball trophies. My picture of Adrian. Over my bed is a painting I did when I was seven. It's a picture of my family. Jake is there. We are all there, and we are all smiling, except for him. I've drawn him really tall and he's wearing blue shorts and a big frown. I fall asleep wondering: What made Jake frown? What made Jake smile?

THREE

I wake at three in the morning. The loss of my friend, Adrian, has become a gaping hole in the pit of my stomach. I go downstairs to the kitchen and try to fill it with food, but that only gives me a stomachache. I return to bed and I lie awake for a long time listening to the quiet of a house lulled to sleep by its own sounds and murmurs. The hum of the refrigerator, the tick of the clocks, the gurgling of water in the pipes. A hundred thoughts pass through my head. A thousand minutes of my life. I think of the people who have come and gone. Grandpa, Jake, now Adrian. In my mind I feel Adrian's rough, calloused hand on my arm. His lips on my cheek. I see his smile. But I know it will fade. As time passes, I will lose the image, the feeling. I will lose him. When my thoughts still, I get up again and walk into the hallway. A memory alights like a gentle butterfly on the edge of my consciousness. I hear my mother's voice, a ghost from the past, "Walk softly, Rachel," she says. It is late afternoon. I am five years old, and I'm wheeling a teddy bear up and down the hall in a baby stroller. Jake is sleeping. My mother passes with a pile of laundry. "Walk softly," she says again. "You'll wake up Jake."

I return to the present. Then I start down the hall. I open the door to Jake's room and I enter. It's hard to believe that in seven years I've never been in this room for more than a few minutes. It's cold and it smells musty. And it's drenched in a quiet like I've never known. I walk over to the bed. In its very center a small circle of light from a streetlamp shines like a halo. I sit down and look around. The room is smaller than I remember it—or maybe I'm just bigger. But it's a boy's room. My eyes wander over each detail of Jake's life. There are posters of the Doors on the wall. Jake liked the Doors, just like me. That makes me smile. A shelf is lined with track-and-field trophies and medals. There are home-built model planes, a rock collection, some camping gear, and a baseball bat in the corner. I am nearly afraid to breathe, to disturb these objects. As I stare at them, they become familiar. They seem to belong here. After all these years I suppose they are at ease and at home. I don't know how long I sit there. Maybe fifteen minutes. Maybe an hour. I feel like speaking, but I don't know what to say. I don't really believe in ghosts, but I feel that maybe Jake can hear me. After a while I whisper, "It's me, Rachel. Rachel three," I add. Suddenly I am filled with sadness. I want to cry, but I laugh instead. I can't help myself. It is the "thing." I hope that Jake is not listening. At last I get up. I leave the room, and as I head back down the hallway, I hear my mother's voice again: "Walk softly, Rachel. You'll wake up Jake."

I go back to my own room and slide between the sheets. I fall asleep wishing that now I could wake up Jake.

By morning it seems like a dream, the evening before, the visit to Jake's room.

Grandma's car is in the driveway. She is in the kitchen with Rachel two. Lately, her visits have become more frequent. She lives alone and I suppose she needs company.

"Rachel," says Grandma. She sets her hands firmly on my shoulders. She is tall like me. All of us Rachels are tall, but I am the tallest. Five foot ten.

Grandma reaches forward and kisses me on the forehead. Her lips are dry and cool.

Rachel two wets a sponge and goes over the counter that Grandma has just wiped.

"They say a cat is good for us old folks," says Rachel one.

"You're not thinking of getting a cat," says Rachel two. She speaks as though Grandma has suggested buying a Ferrari.

"What's wrong with a cat?" I say. But I already know the answer. Rachel two's lips curl inward.

"A cat is a lot of work," she says. "You've got to buy food, change the cat box. Heaven forbid if it gets ill. Now, how are you going to manage that?"

"Heaven forbid if I get ill, you mean," says Grandma. "If I get ill, I can take care of myself. How old do you think I am?" She pauses and waits for an answer.

"Sixty-three," I say. Grandma is in her seventies.

"Don't forget I haven't even started collecting social security." This is not true, but we go along with it, knowing that it makes her feel better. She has been collecting social security ever since she stopped working, ever since Grandpa died. Rachel one used to write an advice column for the local newspaper, which Grandpa founded.

"I used to advise all my readers who lived alone to get a pet," says Grandma.

"Did you advise them what to do when the pet got fleas or kidney stones?" Rachel two asks.

"No," says Grandma. "I left that to the veterinarian who had a weekly column on page three."

Rachel two is silent.

"What other kinds of things did you give advice about?" I ask.

"Everything, honey. From household tips to sex. And my readers listened," she added. "Which is more than I can say for my own daughter."

Rachel one is right. Rachel two is not listening. She has opened a picnic hamper and begun loading it with paper plates and napkins. It's Saturday, and she has organized a family picnic with the Mosers. The Mosers have been a part of our lives forever. Paul went to medical school with Dad, and Betty was Mom's college roommate. They have two children, Bow, whose real name is Bowman, and Priscilla. Bowman Moser's seventeen. His sister, Priscilla, is my age, but we are not really friends. Apart from birthday parties and picnics, we hardly ever see each other.

"Do I have to come?" I ask. Mom frowns.

"Well, it would be nice," she says. "This is a family picnic."

"Don't you want to come?" asks Dad, feigning disbelief. He is rummaging in the hall closet for the softball, bat, and gloves.

"Not really," I say. Rachel two turns to Rachel one.

"Why don't you get some nice house plants?" she

says. "Plants are alive. Plants are good company. And they're easier to care for than a cat."

"I don't have a green thumb like you," says Grandma.

"It doesn't take a green thumb to nurture a few plants," says Rachel two.

Grandma shrugs. "I always told my readers not to get involved in anything they couldn't handle," she says.

Rachel two sighs. She hands me a Tupperware container. I fill it with fruit and snap on the lid just as the Mosers pull into the driveway.

FOUR

Dad and Paul Moser are playing catch with a softball.

"Anyone want to join us?" asks Dad. No one answers. We're each in our own world. The men are acting like boys. Bowman is lying in the grass reading a book. He hasn't looked up since we arrived. Mom and Betty Moser are sitting beneath a tree, deep in conversation. Grandma has strayed from the group and is picking wildflowers. Priscilla is rocking back and forth on a blanket examining her nails, which are painted a peculiar shade of blue. It is obvious that she would rather not be here.

"What time is it?" she asks. She throws back her head and faces the sun.

"I think it must be lunchtime," hints Paul Moser.

"Put on some sun block, Prissy," says Betty. She gets to her feet and begins opening the hampers.

Dad hands around cups of his homemade fruit punch. Its lovely coral color sparkles like the sea at sunset. We stuff ourselves with fried chicken, potato salad, and brownies. The food does something to us. Or maybe it's the punch. Magically, we all begin talking. Bowman starts teasing Dad.

"Pass the salt, Sir John," he says. That's what Bowman calls Dad. It's a play on the word "surgeon." Bowman is making fun of doctors, but I don't think Dad gets it. He is flattered, and I am glad for him.

Dad wants to know what Bowman is reading so intently.

"Organic chemistry," answers Bowman.

Dr. Moser grunts. "I don't believe that for a minute," he says.

"I ought to lend you one of my books," says Grandma.

Rachel two rolls her eyes. "I don't think Bowman is interested in scandalous novels or trashy romances," she says. That's about all Grandma reads these days.

"Sure he is," says Grandma. "Everyone is. Those are the books that tell us about life, about human nature."

"Right, Mother," says Rachel two. She sighs impatiently.

Priscilla turns to me and asks where I got my earrings.

For twenty precious minutes everyone lets go. No time. No space. No nothing. Then something spoils it. It's the way Dad looks at Bowman. With an expression so filled with love and sadness that it makes me want to cry. Then he just sort of leaves us. Mentally, I mean. Just for five minutes or so, but I notice. I realize he's elsewhere. He's with Jake.

Betty, or B.B., as everyone calls her, is the first to mention how late it is. Mom starts collecting paper plates and plastic forks and dropping them in a garbage bag. I snap the lids on the Tupperware containers. Bowman is talking politics with Dad. Suddenly Dad mentions moving.

"Actually, it's Rachel's idea," he adds. He means Rachel two.

"Moving?" I cry. It's the first I've heard of it. Then Rachel two speaks up.

"I just want to make sure Mother has a place she feels is her own." Then she adds, "In case she needs it."

Grandma sticks a bouquet of field flowers in her belt. She takes out a trashy romance and begins reading. Rachel two pretends not to notice.

"She's written me off already," Rachel one says.

"Mom," says Rachel two. "I'm just being realistic."

Dr. Moser shakes his head. "I don't know," he says. "B.B. will tell you. No house is ever big enough."

B.B. protests. "That's not true, Paul," she says.

"Sure it is," says Dr. Moser. "You move to a bigger house because you need more space. Then, as soon as you've moved, you start buying things to fill the space. And before you know it, you need to move again. Believe me. We've moved four times in ten years." He looks at B.B. "And it's never been my idea."

Suddenly I speak up. The idea of leaving my house is unbearable. "We have plenty of space," I say. Everyone looks at me.

"Grandma can go into Jake's room," I add. Priscilla's mouth drops open. Dr. and Mrs. Moser look at each other like I've brought up the dead. I guess I have. Mom and Dad look at the ground. It's Bowman who saves me.

"Did Rachel say something wrong?" he says. That gives me courage.

"Why can't Grandma go into Jake's room?" I say.

Mom is the first to come out of the trance. "Well, I suppose she could," she says. But she is not convinced. Nobody is. But they don't want to talk about it. People can't talk about the dead. It reminds them that any of us could die at any moment. B.B. asks Priscilla to pass her the napkins. Dad puts his arm around me.

"Give me a hand with the blanket," he says. I reach for one end and pull it taut. We waltz forward and backward until the blanket is folded in a neat square.

"You don't really want to move, do you?" I say hopefully. Dad raises his big bushy eyebrows. I used to tug on those eyebrows as a little girl. For the first time I notice they are graying. Dad is looking older. Dad is getting older. He is not willing to take a stand.

"I'm easy," he says. "I'll let you women decide."

We say our goodbyes. Bowman smiles at me. "See you, Rachel," he says. Priscilla says nothing. She is studying her nails again. They have turned a deep purple in the fading light. We all pile into our cars.

"Oh, look," says Rachel two as we pull away from the curb. She's spotted an oriole. We watch it flitter until it disappears. Then she sighs and turns to Dad.

"Can't Paul do something about Bowman's skin?" She's referring to Bowman's acne. "It's a crime he has to go around with all of those pimples on his face."

"He'll grow out of it," says Dad.

"But he'll scar," says Rachel two.

I look out the car window. The wide expanse of green where we were just seated disappears into the distance like a mirage. I have never thought of pimples as a crime. No one is to blame for them. But now that I think of it, life is full of crimes for which no one is to blame.

Dad drops me off at home. He and Mom are stopping by the Mosers' to look at the new patio Paul has put in.

I let myself in the front door and stand in the entrance, motionless. I cannot bear the thought of having to leave this house. It is like I have roots growing from my feet, from the ends of my toes. They have twisted and turned and become embedded in the floorboards. How will I pull them up? How will they survive a transplant?

I hang my jacket on the back of a chair and go to my room. I reach for Adrian's sweatshirt and toss it onto my pillow. Then I lie down on the bed and close my eyes. I try to think happy thoughts about Adrian and all the good times we had. But I am distracted. In my mind, my house rises from the ground and spins through the air out of control. Just like in the movie *The Wizard of Oz*, my life passes before my eyes. All fourteen years of it.

At last I get up. I walk down the hall to Jake's room. I want to ask Jake if it's all right if Grandma comes here. If she takes his room. This time there's enough daylight left to see things clearly. I look at the shelves for so long that everything blurs together. I listen to the quiet. Then everything seems to spring to life. Colors brighten and it seems like I'm seeing them for the first time. I go around the room, and I start to touch Jake's things. At first it feels strange. Then it becomes easy. I pick up Jake's scrapbooks and begin to look through them. They are filled with photos of family, his friends, his track team. There is a picture of him with Mom and

Dad. They look different. Especially Mom. She looks rounder, fuller, and happier. Dad looks more or less the same. Only he's got more hair. Beside the scrapbooks are stacks of papers and notebooks from Jake's school classes. At the bottom there is a book wrapped in a thick gray T-shirt. I lift the book, and the T-shirt falls open. Across the back in big letters is stamped: FRAGILE—HANDLE WITH CARE. This must have belonged to Jake. I refold it carefully and set it on the shelf. Then I take the book and rub my hand along its red vinyl cover. There's no title, so I open it and start to read. It is a journal. It's Jake's journal. This is how it begins.

Once upon a time there was a boy named Jake. He was tall and strong and clever. And he had a nice family who loved him. His teachers loved him, his track coach loved him, his classmates loved him. But he did not love himself. When he saw his face in a window, or in a mirror, he would turn and start to run. Pretty soon he was running all the time, further from home, further from his family, further from life, further from himself.

There are two blank pages and then a second entry.

Once upon a time Jake met a boy named Fisher. Fisher was special. He was different from anyone Jake had

ever met. He did not care how high Jake could jump. How fast Jake could run. He cared how Jake felt.

Hey, Fisher and I were born on the same day. In the same year, practically at the same hour. Dumped into the universe on the same patch of earth. No wonder we get along so well.

I stop reading. I've never kept a journal. I wouldn't know what to write. And I would be afraid that one day someone would find it and read it. I wonder if Jake thought about that. I put the journal down. Maybe Jake wouldn't want me to read it. Then I pick it up again. It's the only way I have to know him. "You don't mind, do you, Jake?" I whisper. He does not answer, but somehow I know he doesn't. I continue reading, and I imagine that he is here on the bed talking with me.

When did I begin to run? Maybe it was that first day of kindergarten when I cried and the teacher called me a baby. I got up and I started to run. I ran out of the room, toward the playground. The teacher came after me and took me back inside, but in my mind I kept on running. And I have been running ever since. I have become good at it, great, in fact. My shelves are lined with trophies and medals. I am fast and I am graceful. But I'm scared, too. I ask myself of what, but I do not

have the answer. Sometimes I wake up at night and I feel my heart beating. I feel the stillness of the room around me. And it nearly smothers me. All I can think to do is run. That's all that will save me. So I lie back down and close my eyes. I imagine myself running, faster and faster until I'm flying, floating, far above the earth, touched only by the wind, the rain that washes me and hides my tears (boys aren't supposed to cry), and the clouds that catch and cushion me as I fall through the air.

I barely hear the car pull into the driveway. Mom and Dad are home. I close the journal, but I do not put it back in its place. I take it to my room, open my drawer, and put it in the space where Adrian's sweatshirt was. For a few short weeks it becomes mine. Jake becomes mine.

FIVE

No one is hungry for dinner. We are all still full of the day and its events. No one mentions moving again. Not even I do. Rachel two escapes to the garden to water the flowers. From the window, I watch her give them their daily pep talk. Rachel two talks to flowers. And when she does, it's as if she opens up and becomes one of them. And I become an alien. Dad is reading the paper and polishing his shoes. He is a master at doing two things at once. It's like each hand has its own brain. I can't even rub my belly and pat my head at the same time. I go to the kitchen and rummage through the refrigerator. I nibble on an apple and yogurt. Then I go to my room to finish my homework.

I am glad to be by myself. Dad is happy to be alone

with his newspaper. And Mom is content to be with her flowers. We need that after an entire day of sharing ourselves.

I lie down on my bed and take out the book I am reading for school. *The Mayor of Casterbridge*. I get through two of the assigned chapters. Although I do not even know these people, I have feelings for them. I find that strange. I close the book, and then I open the drawer of my dresser and reach for Jake's journal. I begin to read silently. I want to read it all at once, consumed by Jake's thoughts and feelings. But I hold back. And I decide to read it slowly, bit by bit, sip by sip, savoring the words. Jake begins to take shape. Soon he is moving with me through a labyrinth of feeling. Though Jake is dead, I begin to see how our lives are intertwined. How something terrible happened to Jake. And how something terrible happened to the rest of us, too.

Hey, it's nighttime. I'm just lying here in bed waiting for the sandman to come. Mom comes by to say good night. "Everything okay?" she asks. I say what I know she wants to hear. "Fine. Everything's fine." I turn toward the window. The moon and stars are coming down to visit me. The sky is black and liquidy, and I'd like to take a run up there. I feel I belong there and not here. Why was I born into this bucket of slop? What am I doing here? Where will I go when it's all over? I can't sleep tonight. I have that electric feeling that moves through my body sometimes. Rachel is crying in the other room. She doesn't want to go to dancing school. Mom is reading her a story. I wish she would read to me. But I'm too old for that.

I don't remember dancing school. Not the teacher, not the lessons. What I remember is standing at the bar in front of a mirror towering over a dozen other girls much shorter than I was. Feeling alone, with my head in the clouds. I remember going home, getting ready for bed, and saying my prayers. I prayed to God that I would stop growing. Then I prayed for a miracle: that I would actually shrink. But it didn't happen. I kept right on growing, and soon it was clear that I would never be a dancer. Still, I didn't give up hope that I wouldn't get any taller. That was my Christmas wish for years. My birthday wish, too. It still is.

I am standing at the window when Dad comes in to say good night. The sky is clear, and the stars are blinking on and off like little traffic lights cluttering the heavens. I am looking for a shooting star.

"Starlight, star bright, first star I see tonight," says Dad. His voice travels across the room and wraps me in its velvety tones.

"What are you wishing for?" he asks. He does not need an X-ray machine to see right through me. "You're wishing you would stop growing," he says.

I shrug. "That, among other things," I say. "I was wishing Adrian were here," I add. It is hard to limit oneself to one simple request. Somehow one wish leads to another. Wishing to be smaller, wishing to stay in this house, wishing for Adrian.

"When you are a surgeon, people will look up to you," says Dad. "You will have the world at your feet," he teases. He knows I will not be a surgeon like he is. Jake did not want to be a doctor either.

"I'm too tall to be a doctor," I say to Dad. "I would frighten my patients."

Now he turns serious. His brow furrows. "Accept it, Rachel," he says. "Save your wishes for things that are possible. Not everything is. Not in this life anyway." He kisses me on the head. Then I catch him glancing at the stars. He, too, like all of us, can't help but wish for things that are not possible.

Mom and Dad are already on my case about college applications. I've got to apply to Dad's alma mater. "Shoo-in." That's what he says, with my grades and my sports ability. Of course, it all depends on what I write on my essay. It's all a joke. If I wrote what I really thought and what I am actually like they'd never take me, except maybe as a specimen for their science lab. So I'll have to do a little comedy here. I haven't told Dad and Mom that I don't want to study medicine. I am afraid they'd choke, and I haven't learned the Heimlich Maneuver. I know they want me to go for that medical degree. To be a surgeon like Dad and fix people up just like new.

What would I like to be? I run from that question, as I do from everything else. Sometimes I think I might like to study English and become a professor. But that thought is buried so deep within my heart that I would have to become a surgeon first and extract it before I could act on it. Besides, only nerds study English. And I don't want to be a nerd.

Fisher thinks that in a previous life I was a traveling bard. Maybe I should write about that on my college applications.

SIX

My birthday's coming up in a few weeks. If I could gather around me all the people in the world born at the same time as me, would I feel like I already know them? Would they be like me? Would they make me feel good the way Fisher does? Could I change their lives? Could they change mine?

"They could," I say softly. I think people can change lives. Adrian changed my life. I am afraid that his leaving will change it yet again. I can no longer recall exactly how I felt the first time I met Adrian. It was more than three years ago. But I know what Jake is talking about. I know the feeling of being with someone who understands you. Someone who knows what you are thinking without your having to speak. Someone who can follow your thoughts and feelings so closely that you feel you are not walking through life alone. Adrian was like that for me. I put on my pajamas and climb into bed. Then I say my prayers. I should be thanking God for health and happiness. But I don't. Instead, I plead with God to let me stay in this house. To bring Adrian back. I finish with "Now I lay me down to sleep." My grandmother taught me that prayer, and I have said it each night since I was a child. Tonight I am joined in chorus by Jake's voice. He knew that prayer, too.

Now I lay me down to sleep, I pray the Lord my soul to keep. And if I die before I wake, I pray the Lord my soul to take. I say this prayer every night. I've said it for so long that I don't really know what it means anymore. I bless my family, my friends, the world. I bless Fisher. It's all show, though. Deep inside I am really praying that I won't go out of my mind, because that's what I so often feel will happen. And for no reason at all. I am not thinking of everyone else in the world. Except to hope that they do not end up like me: a tangled mess of twine. It's a crime.

"It's a crime." It's funny Jake should use those words. Rachel two used them just the other day when she talked about Bowman's pimples. Come to think of it, she uses those words often. She is a blamer. Everything anyone does wrong, every mistake is a crime. "Rachel, it's a crime to leave the bathroom light on. Do you realize how much electricity costs?" It's a crime that I'm not friends with Priscilla Bowman. Of course, that's her job. I ought to forgive her. She's a judge. She is obliged to blame, to decide what is and what is not a crime.

When I wake up, it's Sunday morning. Again I am wearing Adrian's sweatshirt. I put the elbow to my nose and breathe deeply. It still smells of him.

"Who's coming to church with me?" Rachel two wants to know.

Dad declines. He has not been to church for ages. Mom, on the other hand, never misses a Sunday.

"I'll go," I say. I don't want to be charged with another crime. We head down the street. We don't talk about moving. Or the hole in my heart. We talk about the hole in my jeans.

"You've ripped the knee of your pants," Rachel two says. Mentally, she is counting. One, two, three. Three is the magic number. We've made a deal where I've promised to throw out my jeans when I get to the third hole. No patching. No sewing. Three strikes make an out.

"And you could have changed that sweatshirt," she adds.

"I couldn't," I say honestly. I know what she's thinking: It's a crime to go to church in jeans and a sweatshirt. But I am not ready to give up Adrian.

I wonder if *she* knows what *I* am thinking: It's a crime that we aren't able to say what we feel.

We pass the old mill. It's draped in gold, clothed like an icon under the early-morning sun. I am relieved when our thoughts, both of our thoughts, turn to the bread festival, which is coming up.

"Have you decided what you're baking?" Mom wants to know.

"Pumpkin bread," I say. "Remember the recipe that Grandma gave us? The one that belonged to her great-aunt?"

"It sounds delicious," says Mom.

"I've tried making it a couple of times, but I still haven't got the spices right," I say.

"I'll be happy to sample it," Mom offers. She is my best critic. Dad says everything tastes great. Everything is a winner. I have to remind him that there is only one winner. Then Rachel two reminds us both that it doesn't matter who wins or loses. It's how you play the game. I'm not sure I believe that. Jake didn't believe it. I'm not sure anybody does.

The state semifinals are this weekend. I'm running the
100-meter, the 200-meter, and hurdles. All week the

36

coach has been telling me that this is my ticket to college. Meanwhile, Mom has made a point of telling me that it doesn't matter who wins or loses. It's how you play the game. She says this to make me feel better. To give me a cushion should I fall on my face. But it doesn't help. I don't believe it. Losing sucks. It's like being swept into a black hole. The coach starts breathing down your neck and tells you to get your ass in gear. You can't cry. You can't scream. You can't be. O God, dear God, let me win.

I read on, curious to know the outcome of the state semifinals. I find myself rooting for Jake, wanting him to win.

I had a good start and for a few brief seconds I was flying like a bird. All of life was right there before me between the start and the finish line. I was free. I was happy. And I was a winner. First place in the 100 and 200 and second in the hurdles. But it didn't last long. It never does. The crowd stops shouting, the adrenaline drops, and I'm grounded. Back to reality. The coach is yelling, Dad's on my back. God help me!

I am thinking of Jake as Rachel two and I enter the church. We take a seat in a pew near the middle. I look around at the satin drapes. The stained-glass windows like hard candy frozen in a frame. The slippery polished seats of the pews. The robes of the priest. I listen quietly to his sure, silky voice. The words dribble over me like a warm rain. God. God. God. I don't really know who this God is. He has changed over the years. In Sunday school he was the man in the picture book in white robes with long hair. He was the one who knew everything—alongside Santa Claus. For a time he was the man at the corner store who handed out candy to the children on the block. Later he became the crossing guard at school who herded the children safely across the streets. He was Dad prepping for surgery. He was a cloud in the sky with a long cottony beard. He was my volleyball coach when I was chosen for the first team. After Jake died, he became the man at the cemetery, the groundskeeper who mowed the lawns and watered the flowers. Then he lost his form. Now I don't have a clear idea of who or what he is. Neither did Jake.

God help me! Good God! God save the Queen! Who is this guy? Sweet mist that surrounds everyone and everything. Divine being who decides all for us. Good and evil. It's easier to believe that we all came from an amoeba that grew in a swamp. But then we become rather insignificant, don't we? Well, maybe we are. God is handy. Just blame it all on him. Life and death.

God help me. I've stopped going to church. The son of a nice Catholic girl. I've broken my mother's heart. She actually had the nerve to proclaim that as long as I lived in this house I'd be going to church. If she'd just asked nicely I would have gone. But the way she put it I couldn't. I don't mind going. Actually, I rather like it. Staring out the window at the trees. The birds. The pretty stone walls with their cracks and crevices. The drone of the priest is peaceful as long as I don't listen to what he is saying. Why do we have to have an explanation for it all? Can't it just be? Can't I just be without a reason? Can't I just exist without knowing why? Do I have to be judged? God help me. I have stopped going to church. But I can't go to sleep at night without saying my prayers.

SEVEN

Once upon a time there was a boy named Jake. He looked happy. He acted happy. He had a habit of whistling. But inside he was sad and confused. Inside he dreamed of being different. Of feeling different, of feeling good.

Mickey Mouse. That's what we call my chemistry teacher with his big ears and smooth head. Mickey Mouse got me today. He was at the blackboard scribbling away. And I left the room. I didn't really leave, not physically. But mentally I just walked out. I was daydreaming. My mind wandered off, as it has a tendency to do. Wandered right out the door. And it took Fisher with me. We had a run and the blood was flow-

ing and we stopped and we were talking about life and I was feeling happy. That doesn't happen very often. Not in real life anyway. Only in daydreams. And in that second Mickey snapped me back to reality with a question. I wasn't paying attention and couldn't answer. This is about the fifth time that's happened this month. Mickey poked his chem book under my nose and told me to take a big whiff. He kept it there until I inhaled the stale odor of musty textbook. Meanwhile Fish mouthed me the answer. Mickey smiled like Pluto after getting a bone, then went back to the board. But I felt small, really really small.

I am a ball rolled up and small
Bouncing off walls.
Ouch! It hurts.

Here comes the boy with wings.
Is he running or flying?
Strange, you say? Maybe he is an angel
Caught between heaven and earth.
Are those arms or are those wings?
Catch me, I'm falling.
Catch me.
Catch me.
Catch me.

I wonder if daydreaming is a family flaw. Or if it is something everyone does. Right now I am in the kitchen. I am supposed to be setting the table. But I am daydreaming. Dreaming that I am a comedian onstage. Adrian is in the front row, laughing. I can almost reach out and touch him. I want so badly to touch him that my hands become numb. I can barely feel the plates I am holding.

Suddenly Rachel one, Rachel two, and Dad appear in my daydream. They are in the back row. I don't want them to be there, but I can't will them away. They are laughing. Everyone but Rachel two, that is. She is counting the holes in my jeans. I try again to will her out of my consciousness. But she will not leave. I lay the plates on the table. Without thinking, I set one too many places.

"Are we expecting company?" Rachel two asks. She has just walked in the door and put her briefcase down.

"Oh, I wasn't thinking," I say, taking back the extra plate.

"You were daydreaming," says Rachel two. I feel guilty and blush.

"I daydream, too," says Grandma. "Of a nice soft kitten sitting on my lap in my old age."

"Let's not get back onto that subject, Mom," says Rachel two.

"Everyone daydreams," Rachel one continues. And I feel better.

I am glad when the phone rings. "It's for you, Rachel," Mom says to me.

I take the receiver.

"Surprise!" says a voice on the other end. It's Bowman Moser. And it is a surprise. Bowman has never called me before. He barely says hello when we pass in the corridor at school or meet for our family picnics. He has not really paid any attention to me since we were children. He wants to know if I want to go to a movie with him this week. I am flattered.

"Sure," I say. We agree to meet after my volleyball practice on Wednesday. Then I hang up the phone.

"Who else is going?" Rachel two wants to know.

"I don't think anyone," I answer.

"Bowman's seventeen," says Rachel two. "You're only fourteen."

"It's not a date," I tell her.

"Not a date," she repeats. "What is it, then?"

"I remember when Rachel and Bowman used to make snowmen together," says Rachel one. "And mud pies," she adds.

"Wasn't that Priscilla and Rachel?" says Rachel two. She does not remember. At first I don't remember either. Then something jogs my memory. I recall not wanting to play with Priscilla Bowman and her dollhouse. I recall gathering teaberries and decorating the tops of mud pies. Pressing raisins into snowmen's bellies. A shadow is there beside me. It's the shadow of Bowman working silently next to me.

Rachel two shakes her head. "I've forgotten that," she says.

I am struck by how fickle memory is. How we all remember things differently. How we unconsciously alter our thoughts. Or how we forget. I thought I remembered the cold of the snow in my hands as I made snowmen with Bowman. But maybe it is a cold from all the winters that have accumulated in me. I thought I remembered perfectly the color of my first bike. The feel of my first pair of roller skates. My first Halloween. But maybe I am wrong.

Mom is cradling Rachel in the big wooden chair. She is missing Halloween because she's got the chicken pox. I am answering the doorbell and handing out candy to the trick-or-treaters. I greet them at the door, and in my mind I try on each of their guises, searching for one that will make me good. Skeleton, vampire, princess, a monkey. Someone is dressed as a doctor, but I don't even bother to try that one on. The Moser kids have come over. *Priscilla is a black cat and Bowman is a fire-breathing dragon. Mom wants to know if I remember the Halloween when I dressed as a pirate. I don't. She claims to, but the truth is she can't remember, either. That's because we forget everything. There is no retention. Fisher and I were talking about this today. Fisher says that truth is only there for the moment. As time moves on, memory changes and everything becomes a lie. Truth fades like an evening sunset. And we are forced to modify our memory and fill in the details until that becomes our truth. Or just a figment of our imagination. I used to think that the only real truth was in feeling, but now I realize that even feeling is fleeting. It dissipates like a drop of water under the sun. How I long to keep the feeling I felt today sitting on the brick wall next to Fisher listening to the scuffle of the fall leaves. The late autumn sun on the back of my neck. Fisher's voice cracking as he reads me a story that he's written. How I try to hang on to that feeling, but how it slowly creeps away like an animal at dusk. And I am thrust back into the here and now, and Dad, O perfect Dad, is hollering to me to give him a hand with the groceries.*

Dad comes up the driveway. He blows the horn to let us know he's home.

"Why does he always do that?" asks Rachel two.

Rachel one answers. "So you'll know it's only him."

Dad is whistling when he comes through the front door.

"You're in a good mood," says Rachel two.

"That's because I saved not one but two gallbladders today," he says. He kisses both Mom and Rachel one on the cheek. Then he reaches over and kisses my hand, asking if my left cheek is still off limits.

"You're in a good mood, too," he says.

"Rachel's got a date," Mom says.

Dad's brow furrows for a second. My mind travels back to when I was a little girl and he was the one I wanted to marry. I wonder if he is thinking the same thing.

"It's not really a date," I say. "It's just Bowman. He asked me to the movies."

Dad sets his leather bag down on a chair. "Sounds like a date," he says. Then his spirits lift. "Well, I've got myself a date, too." He reaches in his jacket pocket and pulls out some tickets. He hands them to Mom.

"Surprise!" he says. Dad loves surprises. Like me. I love being cornered and startled with, Boo! I love waking up to sunshine when the forecast is for rain. I know there are bad surprises, too, like pop quizzes and chicken pox on Halloween. But I don't mind them.

Mom takes the tickets. They're for the opera. She tries to look pleased. But she is caught off guard. She hates surprises. That is the real reason why Dad blows the horn when he comes up the driveway. No strange car. Nothing unexpected. Jake hated surprises, too.

Surprise! Surprise! Today Mickey popped a surprise quiz on us. I hadn't done the reading, and I handed in a blank paper. It's like dominoes falling. Mickey reminded me that it's going to screw up my average. Then I might get rejected from college and end up dropping out of life. All on account of one chemistry quiz. Surprise! Surprise! I hate surprises. Once Mom threw a surprise birthday party for me. She invited the Mosers, and a lot of kids I didn't really know. I walked in the door and was assaulted. She'd made a cake shaped like a dragon with frosting and candles, and everyone loved it except for me, the birthday boy. After, I had to open my presents in front of them all, nodding and smiling and swallowing the discomfort lodged in my throat.

EIGHT

Lily Rose came by my locker today. Fisher thinks she is beautiful. I suppose she is. But I don't like her. She asks too many questions, and she tries to worm her way inside of me. Today she dangled a key in front of my nose. She said it's the key to her heart. When I said I didn't want it she said, "I know what you're all about." "I don't even know what I'm all about," I said. Then she laughed and began touching my shoulders. Her hair fell into my face and I couldn't breathe. Then her body curved and wrapped around me, and I felt nothing but the Big P—panic! WHAT IS WRONG WITH ME? What is wrong with me! What is wrong with me!

Here is a boy, cold and gray, flattened shiny like a dime.

What is he worth? A cigarette. A pack of gum?
Put him in the vending machine. Look what you
  get. Are you happy now?
No. No.
Take him back. Put him in another time. Are you
  happy now?
A dime is change.
I am strange.

I shower and dress after my volleyball game. Then I wait for Bowman outside the gym. Suddenly I can't remember what he looks like. I close my eyes and try to conjure up his image, but I go blank. When I finally see him, it's as if I'm looking at him for the first time.

"Hi," Bowman says. He drops his head shyly. I've never thought of Bowman as being timid.

"Hello," I say.

"How was the game?" Bowman asks. "Did you win?"

"We did," I say. And I remember my mother's words. "It's not whether you win or lose."

"It's how you play the game," finishes Bowman. "Ya, ya, ya. My mother says the same thing." Then he stops and faces me. "You believe it?" he asks.

"No," I say, shaking my head.

"Me neither," says Bowman.

Bowman and I walk into town. His footsteps move in

unison with mine. They slap the sidewalk at the same time mine do, and that makes me feel good.

I look at Bowman from the corner of my eye. I take in his straight wayward hair that's too long in places. The rough, chapped backs of his hands. His dimples. His pimples. His green eyes. His unbuttoned shirt cuffs and sleeves that are too short. The smell of laundry detergent soaked into his flannel shirt. His perfect square, shining teeth.

We have an hour before the movie begins. Bowman wants to go to the park.

"I have to people-watch," he says. "It's for an English assignment. Do you mind?"

"No," I say.

We sit down on a bench. And before I know it, it's as if we are back making snowmen side by side. Only this time Bowman is talking.

"How was the rest of your day?" Bowman says. He asks in a way that makes me feel that it really matters.

"Good," I say. "And yours?" I ask.

"My day was a usual day. No ups. No downs. An okay day." Bowman nods. He pulls a tablet and pen out of his knapsack and starts scribbling away noisily. I don't have to write, so I can just look. A lady passes with an overloaded shopping cart. She looks haggard and rushed.

"How do you think her day was?" I can't help but ask.

"Hard," says Bowman. He doesn't even look up from his tablet. When he finally does, he looks straight at me. "Life isn't meant to be easy, you know." He's grinning, but a crease in his forehead gives him away. He really believes this.

A woman passes with a carriage and a screaming baby. There are a lot of hurried dog walkers.

"It's weird, isn't it," says Bowman. "These people are passing within inches of each other's heads, completely unaware of one another. That's because they are all thinking different thoughts. Their minds are elsewhere. In their heads some are nearly home. Others have already arrived where they are going."

I nod. Bowman is right. Only the ducks seem here in the present, popping their small heads in and out of the water, searching for bread.

I close my eyes for a moment and wonder if I am in the present. I try to be next to Bowman. To feel the warmth of his body. To listen to his breathing. To be with myself. To feel my own tired muscles. Bowman is right. It is hard, almost impossible. First I am back at school, on the volleyball court. Then I am in the kitchen mixing spices for my bread. Then I am back in my bedroom with Jake.

I could spend hours watching people. I actually do spend hours watching people. Wasting time, my father calls it. I don't think it's wasting time, but I wouldn't dare say that to anyone, except for maybe Fisher. I love to watch the lady in the bread shop wrapping the loaves in that smooth, waxy paper. She's like me. Her hands are there doing the work, but they seem unattached to the rest of her. It's like she's far off, somewhere else. Same with the man tapping his foot as he waits in line at the post office. His foot is there, but his mind is somewhere else. You think I'm here right now, but I'm not. I'm sitting in class. The teacher's taking attendance. She's just put a big check beside my name. She thinks I'm here. The thing is I'm not. My body is here, but I'm long gone. And I won't be back until the bell rings.

We sit in the park watching people weave in and out around us. Watching ourselves. Watching the grass grow. Watching the pavement change color as the shadows lengthen. My eyes return again and again to Bowman's sleeves, shielding those overly long arms that seem to be grasping for something. I will not fall in love with Bowman. I know this from the beginning. You can't fall in love with someone you made snowmen with when you were four years old. With somebody whose parents play croquet in the yard with your parents. You can't fall in love with someone you've known your whole life. The truth is I have never been in love with a boy, not even Adrian. He was my best friend, but I was not in love with him. I thought I was in love with someone in my math class last year. But I was only in love with the way he pushed his hair out of his eyes and the freckles on his elbows. He only ever said four words to me: "You got an eraser?" He passed my locker every day at ten, and he smelled like cherry Life Savers. It's funny how one little thing can make you love someone. Or a lot of little things rolled together in a comforting lump.

Bowman stops writing and puts his pad of paper in his knapsack. He pulls out a pack of matches and begins lighting them and blowing them out.

"Didn't your mother ever tell you that you shouldn't play with fire?" I say, half teasing.

Bowman nods. "She did," he says. "It's a nervous habit. I can't help myself." Then he pulls a book out of his bag.

"What are you reading?" I ask.

"It's a book about reincarnation," Bowman answers. "Do you believe in karma?" he asks.

"What's karma?" I say.

"It's what makes life hard," says Bowman. He laughs. Then he goes on to explain. Bowman believes we've all had many lives. That our spirit lives on somewhere and comes back in other people. All of what we haven't worked out in this life will be met again in another. "That's reincarnation," he says.

"It's nice to think that there's another chance," I say.

"It's not another chance," says Bowman. "It's more like another trial." He lights another match and watches it burn itself out. "Do you ever think about death?" he asks.

"Sure," I answer. I think about people who've died. My grandfather. My brother. "I think about Jake," I say. I don't want to mention his journal, but I ask Bowman if he remembers Jake.

"Yeah," he says. "He was like a god to me. I wanted to be just like Jake. Didn't everyone?"

"Did they?" I ask.

Bowman nods. Then he's journeying back in time, pulling memories from some mental file like news clips.

"The lemonade stand," he says. "Jake made that lemonade stand and set us up in business. That's how I earned my first ten bucks. Dad went around saying I'd be the next Andrew Carnegie." Bowman smiles and then goes on. "I remember Jake's trophy shelf. All those medals. Wow. Then wham!" Bowman slashes the air with his arm. "Blackout. He dies. I kind of lost faith in him after that. I guess that's what happens when your gods die. You realize they are only human."

"I guess so," I say.

"Sometimes I wake up in the night and I will myself to look at death," says Bowman. "To look it in the face. To understand what it will be like to not be anymore."

As Bowman speaks, it occurs to me that when I think about Grandpa and Jake I am not thinking about death. I am thinking about life. And for the first time I wonder where these people have gone. These people I've known and loved. Where will I go? Where will Bowman go? Will we ever stand together again in the same space? Will I meet up with Adrian, Jake, Grandpa somewhere else that's not in a daydream? Or have we been disconnected forever?

Bowman and I end up at a science fiction movie. All the tickets are sold out to the film we want to see. I cannot keep my mind on the screen. I cannot rid my head of what Bowman has said. I can't stop thinking about Jake. He resurfaces again and again like the crest of a wave.

Today I asked Mom if she ever thought about dying. "Oh, Jake," she said. "Whatever made you bring that up?" I didn't have the courage to tell her that I'd spent the night obsessing about death. Driving myself crazy with the thought of my blood slowing in my veins, my breath expiring, and my flesh rotting in the earth. I didn't have the guts to ask her if this was normal. Fisher says it is, but I doubt my mother's ever felt that way. She's the type of person who's eternal. She'll go on forever and she'll never die. What I mean is she won't be any different. Hey, you know what? Maybe she's already dead. I told this to Fish and he laughed. Fisher's got a weird mom. She's some kind of mystic. She's always got a bunch of candles lit, and she makes Fish wear a crystal around his neck. I've only met her once, but I didn't like the way she looked at me with those dark eyes circled by shadows. It was like there was a hole where my navel is and she could see everything that was going on inside of me. Well, I gotta go now. I've got to mow the grass. I promised Mom, and I don't want to let her down.

Bowman walks me home. He reaches in his pocket and pulls out a stone. It's round and smooth.

"I've been carrying it around in my pocket for two and a half years," he says.

"I don't believe you," I say.

"It's true," says Bowman. "It started as an experiment. It's gone through the wash a hundred times. And it's continually rubbed against my thigh. Look how smooth and round it's become." He hands me the stone. It is small and compact, warm and heavy. I look at Bowman doubtfully.

"Really," he says. "Cross my heart. Keep it if you want," he adds. He does not wait for me to reply. He kisses my cheek and says good night. Then he asks if I want to do something again.

"Okay," I say. I watch him walk away. From behind I see a gentleness in his movements, in the curve of his back, that is not visible from the front. He strikes another match. The flame jumps to light in the settling darkness and gives the illusion of welcome into a place that has no entry.

Rachel two is in the kitchen at the sink, slicing apples.

"I'm home," I say. But she doesn't answer. She doesn't seem to hear me. She is scattered. Her hands are slicing, going through the motions. But none of her is there. For the first time I realize that a part of her has not been there for a very long time. I could walk through her. I could take the knife from her hand and she would not have the power to retrieve it. She is looking out the window into the garden. Then her gaze moves past the trees and back through time. She is like the people I saw today in the park. Visible to the eye, but not really there.

I've finished mowing the lawn. Razed nice and neat like an emerald bed. Tomorrow morning the dew will sparkle like a jeweled crown. Only trouble is I got carried away or distracted by those shaved green spears tickling my ankles, and I chopped off the heads of the crocuses. Mom choked and roared until I thought the roof would fall in. And I felt like crap. Geez, I really am sorry. I said so. She was as mad as a raging bull. Then I got angry and said why didn't she just call in Dad to patch things up. That's his specialty: putting people back together. He could certainly sew the heads back on a few flowers. She said I was being arrogant and contemptuous. I told her she should have been an English major. That shut her up. Later I went back to the garden. I stood over those crocuses. And I felt sad I'd done that. Mom found me there and she hugged me from behind. She said no one's perfect. But that's not true. She is perfect. Dad is perfect. Why can't I be perfect, too?

Dad comes into the kitchen. He washes his hands. "I'm hungry," he says and opens the refrigerator. "How was your date?" he asks.

"It wasn't really a date," I say.

"How was the board meeting, then?" he jokes.

"Do you always have to tease?" Rachel two asks. She

is back with us now, handing Dad a slice of apple. Dad always does have to tease. It keeps him from saying what he really feels.

"All right, all right. What did you guys do?" Dad asks.

"We watched people," I say. "For a paper Bowman is writing for English class. And we saw a bad movie." I empty my gym bag and carry the clothes into the laundry room off the kitchen. Dad follows me. He picks up a sock I've dropped. I toss my dirty wash into the machine. But I am not really here. I am back with Bowman, watching people who aren't really there, talking about life and death.

I look over at Dad. "How does it feel when a patient dies?" I ask.

The space around us expands, and I can feel him here beside me when he answers.

"It feels awful, Rachel," he says. "And worse because often the patient does not know. There are no real goodbyes. And you're surrounded by strangers." Dad is suddenly caught up in the cloud of death. I want to rescue him.

"Don't forget all the lives you save," I say.

"That's the trouble, Rachel," he says. "It's all too easy to forget when life and death are reduced to a blip on the EKG machine." He pauses and then continues.

"Today I left two patients on the table to be stitched

up," he says. "I don't know if they made it or not." For a second Dad is back at the hospital in the operating room. "I left them sleeping peacefully," he says.

"I'm sure they're okay, Dad," I say. The sadness is not allowed to surface. Rachel two breaks into the conversation. "Remember, you're not God," she calls from the kitchen. She defends him and absolves him like a good judge. She says it calmly and objectively, with no emotion. This is what she's trained to do.

Dad goes to Mom. He places a hand gently on the back of her neck. "How was your day?" he asks. Again I think of Bowman.

"A lot of parking ticket contestations," says Rachel two.

It occurs to me that we've all asked each other about our day. But no one has asked about us. No one has said, "How are you?" We have all spoken through our experiences. I look closely at my parents. Each of them. Dad is tired and sad. Mom looks angry somehow. And me? How do I look? I go into the bathroom and gaze into the mirror. At first I look happy. I am happy. About the game. About Bowman. But as I keep looking, the lines and shadows become visible. It is all there. I am sad about Adrian. Angry at the idea of moving. Angry about being so tall.

I take the stone that Bowman gave me from my

pocket, and I put it in the dresser alongside Adrian's sweatshirt and Jake's diary. There is also the ticket from my first helicopter ride, the shirt from my first year of volleyball. I am touching these moments that have passed when I hear the phone ring. It's the real estate agent. She has another property for Rachel two to look at. This worries me. Suddenly I am aware of a strange hush, like a secret lodged within the walls and under the floors. This house, like us, has feelings and emotions stashed away, buried deep. Somewhere there is a lot of pain. I am afraid that when we move and shake things up, it will all surface.

Once there was a boy named Jake. Some people are born with too many fingers or too much hair. Jake was born with too many feelings.

I am sitting at my desk tapping my pencil. My legs are bouncing up and down. "Stop fidgeting, Jake." Mom's voice resounds in my head like a broken record. She might as well say, "Stop feeling, Jake." It's feelings that make me fidget. I don't know what to do with them. I try to shove them away somewhere, under the carpet, the pillow, but there are too many of them. I don't know how to express them, so they come out as fidgeting. People with feelings fidget. Isn't that right, Mom?

It snowed last night. There was a cool crisp blanket covering the earth. But then the trees started to move and shake the weight off their back. Icicles dripped and glistened in the sunlight. And warmth began to radiate from the snowbanks. I stopped and stripped and dove into the pond where the ice had given way. The cold hurt. But then I went numb and it was okay. Fish followed me, and we swam for five long minutes.

The snow is falling in thin-spun flakes.
Tapping my shoulder. Melting into my skin.
A white bright message from the heavens
    reminding me of infinity.
The ice is thawing.
Around me it melts and runs into a puddle
    alongside my tears and my sweat.
And they merge together into a stream, flowing
    toward the river and back into the earth.

I go to sleep thinking of my day. Holding on to it. I don't want tomorrow to come. I don't want Rachel two to see that house. I think of Bowman. In a moment somewhere between reality and sleep I see a fire. All of the keepsakes in my dresser are dancing around it. But they are untouched. And I am looking in the mirror and feeling happy. *Really* happy.

It is winter. The animals have grown a thick coat of fur and have gone to sleep. It is the long night for them. When they wake, it will be like starting a new life. I would like to go to sleep in the deep dark of winter and wake to sunshine and flowers. It must be like being reborn.

Oh, life is a deep sleep. The man on the bus is snoring. The world is passing him by. He is happy. He has a smile on his face. Life is a sweet sleep.

NINE

WALK SOFTLY, RACHEL

Before I know it, tomorrow is today. I am at the kitchen table doing my homework. Rachel two went to see the house, and she loves it.

"The garden was lined with the most beautiful lilies in bloom," she says.

"You could plant lilies here," I say.

"Rachel, you can't resist change," she says. "Change is part of life. Letting go is part of life."

"I don't want to move," I say. "I'm happy here."

"You'll be happy somewhere else," says Rachel two.

"What if I won't," I say. The whole scenario unfolds in my head. A new house means starting all over. A new room. A new smell, new space to get used to moving around in, bumping into things. I don't want that. I like walking into my own room, eyes closed, and knowing how things belong, smell, without even touching them. Our spirits have melted into this house, and I don't want to leave it. But I know when my mother's mind is made up. I can already hear the hollow echo of my own footsteps as I take the stairs up to my room. The banister is cold. Or maybe it's my hands that have become cold. The spirits are already being laid to rest. I pass Jake's door. And I hear myself sigh. I hear Jake's voice in my head and I know Rachel two is right. Change is letting go. It's breaking attachments. It's goodbye.

Leaves change, seasons change, a chameleon changes color, people change. People are changing all the time. They change their minds. They change the color of their hair. They change their clothes. I wish I could change. I wish I could be peaceful, still, and happy. But each time I get there, I barely settle into the feeling when wham, along comes Mr. Change with his baggage of worry, confusion, doubt, and agitation. And he dumps it on me. No wonder I am afraid of change. Maybe Fisher is right. He says the only true stillness is when the breath ceases forever and the limbs stop twitching.

Mom and Dad were leaving this weekend with Rachel for the mountains for three days. And now they've changed their minds. Too bad. Fisher and I had a great weekend planned. Beers, movies. Without Mom hanging over me like a palm frond. Now she's changed her mind. I think it's because of me. She says she doesn't want to leave me alone. I don't know if I want to be left alone or not.

TEN

I am with Bowman. I am helping him choose a birthday present for his sister. I take him to the store where I bought my earrings, the ones Priscilla liked. He lingers a long time before choosing a pair. I am surprised and touched by this. I am surprised, too, by the amount of time I am spending with him. Slowly, he is stepping into Adrian's shoes.

Bowman pays for the earrings and slips them into his shirt pocket. Then we stop at the drugstore for a birthday card.

"Do you want a coffee?" Bowman asks. He takes a seat on a revolving stool. I sit next to him.

"No, thanks," I say. "I don't like coffee."

Bowman asks for two. "Very black," he says. He drinks them down one after another.

"Are you sure you ought to drink so much of that so fast?" I say.

"You sound like Luci," he says. Luci was Bowman's girlfriend. They were together for two years. Now they've split up. Bowman is heartbroken. I can tell. But he doesn't want to talk about it, other than to say that Luci left him and she didn't say why.

Bowman crunches up his empty paper cups and tosses them in the garbage. I follow him out of the drugstore. We head for the river. All of a sudden Bowman stops and looks at me. "You're really tall," he says.

"I am," I say. "Did you just notice?"

"Yes," he says, nodding. "You never seemed that tall. It must be sort of nice to be so tall," he adds.

"It has its advantages," I say. I list them. "You look older. You can get into adult movies. People expect more from you. You become a professional reacher. You stand in the back of all lines. It's a scream," I say.

Bowman laughs. "Sounds it," he says. Then he becomes serious. "Can I ask you something?"

"Sure," I say.

"You promise not to laugh," he says.

This is a hard promise for me to keep. Bowman does not know about the "thing." No one does, except my family and Adrian. Adrian was the only friend I ever told. "Is it something sad?" I ask.

"No," says Bowman.

"Okay, I promise," I say.

"Does it bother you to look at my pimples?" Bowman asks. "Do you find them horrible and offensive and disgusting?" He grins. I am not sure if he is serious or not.

"I don't mind them," I say. This is true. "They don't really bother me. I hardly notice them anymore."

"Do you know how many jokes there are about pimples?" he says. "Run for cover. A volcano is erupting next to you. Hey what kind of pizza do you want? I know, pepperoni, to match your face." Bowman laughs. "Double, double, toil and trouble. Pimple burst, and pimple bubble."

I want to laugh. But I feel the tears well up in my eyes and I cover my face.

"Rachel, you're crying," says Bowman.

"No," I say. But I cannot hide the tears that are streaming down my face. "I'm laughing."

"It looks to me like you're crying," says Bowman.

I try to explain. "I have this 'thing,'" I say. "This defect. I laugh when I want to cry and I cry when I want to laugh. It's been like that ever since I can remember."

"Really?" says Bowman. "That's amazing."

I start to laugh. Then the tears take over. "You see?" I say. "If you take me to the saddest movie in the world,

I'll burst out laughing and everyone will look at me like I'm a freak."

"Sorry, that's not good enough to be a freak," says Bowman. "You've got to have tons of ripe squishy pimples on your face to be a real freak." I cry even harder.

We sit down on the bank of the river that flows past the mill. The wildflowers are coming up. Bowman pulls out a pack of matches and starts lighting them randomly.

"What is it with you and fire?" I ask.

Bowman shrugs. "I don't know," he says. "I like the warmth. I'm always cold." He gives me his hand. It's like ice.

"I like to watch the colors. See?" he says. He lights a match and sets fire to the sales receipt from Priscilla's present. Streaks of blue, orange, and yellow shoot into a flame. Then it burns itself out. Bowman is entranced. "It's incredible, isn't it," he says.

"It's dangerous, Bowman," I say. But he doesn't get it.

He lights another match and stares into the flame. "A caveman walked out of his cave one day after a lightning storm. He saw a tree burning. He was frightened, but he was attracted by the warmth. He moved closer, basking in the radiant heat. Then it began to rain. And the fire went out." Bowman frowns.

"Is that a true story?" I ask.

"I read it in a book," says Bowman. "I read a lot."

"I know," I say.

Bowman is looking at me. His gaze cuts right through to my center. "What are you thinking about?" he asks.

"My grandmother's birthday," I say. "It's coming up, and she wants a cat. I'd like to get her one, but my mother's against it. She hates cats." Then I'm thinking out loud. "I might just get her one anyway," I say.

"I don't know if I'd do that," says Bowman. "But it's your choice."

I listen to Bowman, but I don't really feel that I have a choice.

Today Mickey was telling us that life is a choice. He says it's like that right from the beginning. You can choose to breathe or not to. I have the choice of being a doctor or a scholar or a bum. I have the choice of being a winner or a loser. It does not matter what anyone else thinks. I must block all that out. The problem is I can't. It's all the Big B—bullshit! There are no choices. I feel like if I hold my breath for long enough I'll pass out and then I'll start breathing again.

Bowman and I walk through town toward home. The stores are bustling with activity. A banner is spread across the road announcing the bread festival. It's coming right up. I've not been keeping track of time.

"Are you baking something?" I ask Bowman.

"I am," he answers proudly. "Grapefruit peel bread. It's my own recipe."

"Really?" I don't know whether to believe him or not.

"Yes," he says.

"It sounds great," I say.

"And you?" Bowman asks. "What are you concocting?"

"I'm not telling," I say. "I never let on before the moment of truth."

Bowman smiles. "Fair enough," he says. "Anyway, I like surprises."

"Me too," I say. And I think of the day Bowman called me for the first time.

When I get home I find Rachel one in the kitchen making cornbread. Rachel two is in her study doing her accounting. I pull my pumpkin bread recipe out of a recipe box. Rachel one speaks up. She does this a lot lately. Just picks up the threads of her life and begins talking. I guess it's because she's growing older.

"I married the boy down the road," she says. "He was delivering newspapers. Up at five and out on his bicycle. I loved to see him cruising down the street, the sun just coming up. When he died, that's what I remembered most. He had something about him even then. He wanted to be a newspaper man and I knew he would. All that he would become was in him even then. I wonder if that's true of us all?" She pauses and looks out the window. Then she continues. "I never had another man, but times have changed. People are more demanding, and well they should be." Grandma sighs.

"Do you remember kissing Grandpa for the first time?" I ask.

"I do," says Grandma. "I remember how good it felt." She turns to me. "So tell me about that Moser boy," she says.

"You mean Bowman?" I ask. "What do you want to know?"

"Have you kissed him?" Grandma asks.

"No, he's just a friend," I say.

"You have a lot of them, Rachel, before you choose," she says. "You try them out just like you would a new car. That's what I say."

"What are you telling her, Mother?" Rachel two's voice drifts over from across the hall. "In this day and age."

"I'm telling her the truth, honey," says Rachel one. "That's all that matters."

"I thought Bowman had a girlfriend," says Rachel two.

"Bowman did have a girlfriend," I say. "But they

broke up. It's been really hard on him. He really loved her."

"He'll get over it," says Grandma. "He needs time to lick his wounds. If you only knew the number of letters I've answered about broken hearts."

"What do you say?" I ask. "What is there to say?"

"I tell the truth, Rachel," Grandma answers. "Broken hearts are part of life. Just like broken glass and blown-out tires. If you can get on and keep breathing, it will heal. The trick is in the breathing. If you stop breathing, you're finished."

Rachel one pulls a large envelope out of her bag. It's filled with newspaper clippings, stiff and yellowed with age.

"Look what I found," she says. "These are all the recipes we received at the newspaper. At festival time we used to get everything. You would not believe what landed on my desk."

I start going through the recipes in the envelope. Wishbone bread, onion skin bread, pineapple loaf. Grandma dips her hand into the flour bin. It was she who taught me to make bread. She has always come over on Sundays and baked. I would watch her swaying forward and back as she kneaded the dough. And after it had risen, she would let me punch it down. Then it would rise again and we would knead in raisins, nuts, olives, dried fruit. After, we would braid it or coil it and slip it into the oven. And I would watch it rise in the small glass window of the stove as it baked.

"Your mama used to make the nicest bread," Grandma says. "Then she lost interest and took up gardening."

I do not remember Rachel two ever making bread. I cannot imagine it either. I try to picture what it would be like to see her there in an apron with her hands white with flour. But in my mind I can't take off her judicial robes.

Mom is down in the kitchen making my favorite bread, cinnamon swirl. I love watching her knead the dough and seeing it swell and clutch the sides of the greased bowl. She always lets me punch it down before the final rising. I give it a smack and we smile. The smell is creeping up the stairs and into my room. It wakes me from my reverie and I go down to the kitchen to wait for Fisher. Together we finish off a loaf. Mom says, "Easy, fellows," but I see that she's pleased. The bread festival is coming up. She'd like me to make something. Maybe I'll humor her and do it this year. I could go through the motions. I could get up with the birds and strap an apron to my waist. Then I could sprinkle,

*mix, and measure, breathing in the odor of flour and
yeast. I could knead the dough with my very own hands
and feel life flowing to my fingertips. Then, as day
draws to a close, I could march through town with my
loaf held high. And for one day of the year, one day of
my life, I might feel like I belong, truly belong. Why
don't I do it? Because I am afraid of failing. Of disappointing everyone. Of disappointing myself.*

Rachel one mixes the dough. She gathers it into a ball
and begins kneading. She hums to herself as she works.
I am reminded that her birthday is coming up.

"How old are you going to be this year, Grandma?" I
ask. "Tell me the truth."

Her eyes sparkle. "Seventy-eight," she says. She's
looking forward to it like a child. It is so very different
from Rachel two, who, every year, ducks her birthday
like a cunning dodger.

"I hope you're going to make my favorite cake,"
Grandma says.

"You bet," I say. "Anything else you want, besides
that?" I ask.

"I told you what I want," she says. "World peace.
Everyone to be happy. A cat." Then she stops kneading
long enough to smile at me. "Is that so much?" she asks.

"No, Grandma," I say.

Rachel two comes into the kitchen. "Mother, you can't have a cat," she says.

"A nice warm bundle for my lap," says Grandma.

"You're daydreaming," says Rachel two. "This is real life. You don't need another mouth to feed. Another someone to take care of."

"Real life?" says Grandma. Then she begins to ramble again. "I guess it is," she says, her voice fading. "Real life is the school of hard knocks. In real life people lose the ones they love. Just look at Bowman. In real life people get hurt and die. In real life people are not always rewarded for their good deeds and punished for their crimes. Isn't that so, Rachel?" I do not know if she is talking to Mom or to me.

"That's right, Grandma," I say. "In real life beanstalks do not climb up to the sky and finish in a pot of gold."

ELEVEN

Today Fisher's grandfather had a heart attack. The doctor says he's half-dead.

"What's half-dead?" I ask.

"I dunno," said Fisher. "What do you think?" Fisher is always asking me what I think. He started crying and I wanted to put my arm around him. But I didn't dare and I hated myself for that.

Fisher said his grandfather has already written his epitaph. Just like in the Spoon River Anthology, where all the villagers in a small midwestern town have died and written their own epitaphs. Maybe everyone should write their own epitaphs, how they want to be remembered. Maybe it would help them to live. Fisher and I talked about how we wanted to be remembered.

Fisher said he didn't care as long as it wasn't as Fisher
Cox the THIRD. He hates being named after his father
and grandfather. He says they did that to him so that
when they died they could go on living through him. I
told him it didn't matter. I wasn't named after my
parents, but I still feel like they want to go on living
through me. Then Fisher said he just wanted to walk
through life anonymously. Fisher is so humble. I love
that about him. I don't know how I want to be remem-
bered. Maybe simply as human. Someone who made
mistakes. Who was good and bad.

I have never minded sharing my name with my mother
and grandmother. I have never thought of them dying
and living on in me, but I like the idea of a small part of
their spirit taking refuge in my bones. I can only hope
to be remembered as Rachel three. But I am afraid I
will be remembered as a string bean. We are studying
metaphor and symbolism in English. Our assignment is
to write a paper describing ourselves as a vegetable or
fruit. I could only be a string bean. It is the one vegetable or fruit long and skinny enough and knobby at
the joints.

As I write, everyone in my life becomes a vegetable
or fruit. Dad is a furry peach with his bushy eyebrows
and soft sweetness. Rachel two is an eggplant shriveled

by the sun, lined and puckered. That nice green stem and collar remind me of her judicial robes falling over her shoulders. But she is bitter close to the skin. I taste that sometimes. Rachel one is like a cucumber, cool and fresh and seedy, with dry rough skin and mellow yellow pulp. I think of Adrian. I still think of him at least a dozen times a day. He is an apple, familiar, and sweet, with crunchy skin that you can eat. This makes me smile. Bowman is a tomato. He needs a lot of sunshine and heat. I can't help but think of his pimples, like squashed tomato pulp. My volleyball teammates are all string beans like me, reaching for the sky.

If Adrian were here, we'd be doing our papers together and we'd be laughing. Well, I'd be crying. I'm crying now, though it comes out as laughter. That's because I miss Adrian. I take his sweatshirt out of the dresser drawer and hold it. It's cool and it still smells of him.

"Adrian apple," I say. I remember what Grandma said about breathing. I stop breathing when I think of Adrian. It hurts to breathe and think of him at the same time. But I want life to go on. I try to inhale, ever so slightly, while I am thinking of Adrian. I do this a hundred times. Somehow for a second I feel closer to him. Adrian. I wonder how he remembers me.

I look out the window at the neighborhood children playing ball in the backyard, and my English paper floats away. The vegetables shrivel up and die. I look at Jake's journal spread open on my desk, and a memory comes back to me. I, like Grandma, wanted a cat when I was small. I begged for one for my birthday. But Rachel two would not get one for me. Suddenly her voice is chiming in my ears. "A black cat means bad luck. Curiosity killed the cat . . ."

Rachel got me two gerbils instead. I remember those gerbils. I had them for two years. Then they disappeared. Jake told me that during the night they had escaped to the garden. He said they wanted to live there among the colorful blossoms and the damp, cool earth. I spent hours looking for them in the shadows, in and among the rocks and flower beds. Jake kept saying that they were hiding because they didn't want to go back in the cage. He said they were glad to be free and that I should be happy for them. Suddenly my memory reaches a dead end. When I pick up its threads, the gerbils have died of sunstroke. But I keep on believing that they are alive and happy in the garden. When did I stop believing? When did I know they had died?

Twelve

I meet Bowman after volleyball practice. This has become a habit. We begin walking toward nowhere in particular. Bowman lights up a cigarette. It's the first time I've seen him smoke.

"Didn't your dad ever show you those pictures of burnt-out lungs?" I ask. My dad has shown them to me a dozen times.

"Sure he did," says Bowman. "Don't all doctors do that to their kids? And for those whose dads aren't doctors, there's the science museum. It scared the daylights out of me. I'm not really smoking," Bowman goes on. "I'm just letting the cigarette burn down in my hand. I like the way it feels. The warmth as it moves closer to my skin."

Bowman flicks his cigarette, and ashes float languidly

to the ground. I watch the glowing butt consume its white paper casing. It seems almost alive. But I cannot rid my mind of the images of charcoal-stained lungs. Of the idea of death.

Rachel is singing in her room. She's playing ring around the roses with her dolls. "Ring around the roses, a pocket full of posies. Ashes, ashes, we all fall down." She is laughing. She thinks the song is simply about flowers. But she is wrong. I just read about that song in a history book. It was a chant from the Middle Ages at the time of the Black Plague. A red rash around the neck was the first sign of a victim. Sweet-smelling flowers were stuffed in his pockets to conceal the putrid smell of the disease until the victim fell down—dead! Isn't innocence beautiful? Maybe death is beautiful, too. But we have made it out to be shameful.

I lost the game.
I feel lame.
What a shame.

Shame is an awful word. It's an awful feeling.

Bowman tosses his cigarette into a puddle. It fizzles and smokes and dies out.

"I suppose you wanted to be a fireman when you were a little boy," I tease.

Bowman nods. "I did," he says. "And I wanted a dog named Spot to ride beside me up front there in the engine."

"I wanted to be Alice in Wonderland," I say, "so I could eat a mushroom and become smaller." I sigh. "Now I know that's not possible."

"It's funny how the world changes," says Bowman. "How we change. When you were little, didn't you always want to be grownup?"

I nod, and Bowman goes on.

"Then, as you get older, you realize that adults are nothing special. They are just people. We are all just people."

Bowman is graduating from high school this year. "So you still want to be a fireman?" I say. He shakes his head.

"What do you want to do?" I ask.

"I want to take a year off and maybe work in a factory. Then I'll go to college. My parents want me to go to college right away. They're worried that if I take a year off, I'll take my entire life off."

"You're not going to be a doctor like your dad," I say.

"No," says Bowman. "I'm not going to be a doctor. Actually, I'd like to be a professional reader." He laughs. "So, if you know of any openings . . ." He lights up another cigarette. "Actually, I have no clue what I want to do," he says. "And it drives my parents crazy," he adds.

"Lots of people don't know what they want to be at your age," I say. I am thinking of Jake.

Once upon a time there was a boy named Jake. He felt like Chicken Little. He felt the sky was falling.

What is Jake going to do with his life? That's the million-dollar question. It's hanging off everyone's lips. Today I told a friend of Mom's that I was going to be a traveling bard, and I watched her mouth fall open. What the hell does it matter to her what I want to be? I just want to be normal. I just want to seek refuge in unconscious, effortless monotony. This morning I woke up and I just wanted to go back to sleep. Forever.

I realize Bowman will be leaving in a few short months. Like Adrian. And I stop breathing.

"What about you?" Bowman asks. "Ever think what you want to do?"

"I'd like to be a comedian," I say. "I'd like to make people laugh."

"You make me laugh," says Bowman.

"I'll have to repair this defect," I say, "before I can do it. Otherwise I'll be crying all the time."

"There must be some pill or something you can take," Bowman says.

"There isn't," I say.

"Maybe I can fix it," says Bowman. He tickles me in the ribs. I try to laugh, but then the tears come to my eyes.

"It's not that easy," I say.

"What about this?" says Bowman. He puts a stick of grape gum in his mouth and begins to blow a giant bubble. It pops in his face. I want to laugh, but the tears continue to flow down my cheeks.

I leave Bowman at the library. That's his second home. He has some books to drop off and he wants to borrow some more. On the way home I stop by Dad's office. I haven't done that for a long time. I used to like to go there when I was small. He would take me with him on the weekends. I would play with the skeleton on his shelf, the knee joint, the model of a heart, and do drawings while he spent hours going over his journals, writing articles, studying his patients.

The nurse and the receptionist have left and Dad is alone, bent over his desk, recapping the day.

"Hi, sweet pea," he says. "This is a pleasant surprise." Then he looks worried. "What brings you here? Something wrong?"

"No," I say. "I was just feeling nostalgic. I was thinking about how I used to come here when I was little."

"And turn the X-ray light on and off," says Dad.

"And play with the skeleton and wonder how all those little pieces fit together and worked. Or didn't, as the case may be."

Dad grins.

"Remember when we used to play Operation?" I say. "That game where we had to remove bones from a patient with tweezers without the buzzer going off?"

"I sure do," he says. He holds an X ray up to the light box. "Look at this. A gallstone the size of a walnut. And shaped like one, too." He studies it for what seems like an eternity. And I think to myself, here is a man who really loves his work. When he finally puts the X ray down, I know what he will say.

"Isn't the human body an amazing machine." It's not the first time I've heard him say this.

"Did you always want to be a doctor?" I ask.

He nods. "Ever since I was a little boy," he says. "When I was a child, I used to go around patching up the neighbors and their pets. Then when I was a teenager, the highlight of my summer was catching frogs and beetles and dissecting them on the picnic table, much to my mother's horror." He takes another X ray from his desk and clips it onto the light box. "What's this?" he asks, pointing to a long thin bone.

"Ulna," I say.

Dad nods proudly. Over the years he has taught me the name of nearly all the major bones in the body. I stand up and walk over to the model of a skeleton exhibited on a shelf. I dangle its legs. Then I focus on the anatomy chart and the tray of sterile instruments. I am touched by all of these props and how they define the identity of my father.

"You're lucky," I say. I see he has been traveling the same path ever since he was a child. He had direction. I see how hard it is for Bowman, who has no direction. And I think how hard it was for Jake, who was lost at a crossroad.

"I know," says Dad. "I am lucky."

I passed by the Père's office today. I needed some cash for a new bike tire. He handed it over, no questions asked. I have to hand it to him. He is generous and trusting. He pulled the old X-ray trick again. Pointing to a bone. "What kind of a break?" he asked. "Boot top fracture," I say, and he grins from ear to ear. There is a heart beating on the shelf. I do not have the heart to say that I hate this room. The smell of alcohol and disinfectant. The bare bones of it all, shall we say. My heart does not beat to be a doc like his. God, how I wish it did. Dad does not see this. Although I have no medical degree, I diagnose him as partially blind. We do not look each other in the eyes. We stopped doing that a long time ago. It is too hard to see his aspirations for me lurking behind those purple irises. Too painful for him to see my doubts, hesitations, fears. I wish I could be a doctor for him. But I know, and he knows, that I would break and there he would be, sweeping up pieces of me off the lab floor. I look at all the eager faces in the waiting room ready to put their lives in his hands. Those strong, sturdy, square-nailed hands that were the first to touch my naked skin. I can still feel the imprint as though it were yesterday. Now I'll tell you a funny thing about my skin. It is smooth and seamless. I have no freckles, no marks, except that birthmark which Moser removed. I have not one pimple. Or a scar from a scratch or a skinned knee. I am flawlessly sewn together. Inside I am sure that I am filled with pimples. With scars and bleeding wounds that have grown inward. You just cannot see them. Nobody sees them. And nobody feels them but me. I wonder if I would see them on an X ray. If I would see that I was sewn together wrong with my skin turned inside out and all the nerve endings exposed.

Mrs. Grebble with her gnarled arthritic hands comes in from the waiting room. Dad has helped her to touch and feel and hold for years. And she looks at him with love and reverence.

"You remember Jake, my son," he says.

"Of course I do," says Mrs. Grebble. And she gives me a gnarled hand.

"What a handsome boy," she says. And Père's eyes are glowing, and Mrs. Grebble and I are there standing before our creator. She cannot see the inside of me. But I've told you what it's like. I'd better stay clear of that X-ray machine or everyone will know.

As we are leaving, I take a final look at the X-ray box and I can't help but think of all the things inside of us that you cannot see in those pictures.

THIRTEEN

WALK SOFTLY

My seventeenth birthday is coming up. Right around the bend. Zooming toward me. I hear its drone from afar. It hums gently, then gets louder.

I wake up and it's here. It's my birthday, and my parents have given me a car. Can you believe that? A cute little blue sports car. I never did like the color blue. Aren't boys supposed to like blue? Aren't they born with a blue ribbon around their ankles? And girls a pink one. I never liked cars as a little boy either. I guess they have forgotten that. I had a nice set of Matchbox cars. Someone was always adding another. I had every type and color parked under the bed. Then one day I made a junk yard and scrapped them in the backyard. Anyway, I gaped at the car, slapped her fender, and called her Claire, and it was like I made love to her. I slid into the driver's seat and turned on the engine, pumped the gas, and tried her out. I drove around the block half a dozen times. Then I swung back into the driveway and parked her in the garage. "It's just what I wanted," I managed to spit out. Then I spit in the driveway. Dirty words. I hate to lie. The lie grows bigger and bigger right before my eyes. My nose is growing longer and longer. And there's a big headlight on the end of it. Never tell a lie. Isn't that a cardinal rule? And here I am with my nose two miles down the road. Aren't I lucky? My mother says that a hundred times a day. Well, I am. My dad is a surgeon. He can cut off this nose and make things right. But will they ever be right?

Fisher came by later. It was his birthday, too. His father had completely forgotten and his mother had given him another crystal to wear around his neck. I gave Fish a cookbook. He loves to cook. We went down to the basement and played a few rounds of pool. We had a couple Cokes and laughed a lot. Fisher told me about the birthday parties his mother used to throw for him. Or, I should say, the ones she didn't throw. Fisher has never had a party. Can you believe that? It hurts. I could see it on his face, and I wanted to cry for him. I *love Fisher, the scars on his knees, the pimples on his face, all of his imperfections. I wish I could walk into him, pass through his soul, feel how he works. Starlight, star bright, first star I see tonight . . .*

Jake aches. Jake forsakes. Jake makes a cake for Fisher. Jake fakes. Jake wakes feeling sad. Jake makes mistakes. Jake breaks. Oops.

I am in the kitchen with my mother. She is cutting back the stems on the ivy. I am unloading the dishwasher, but my mind is elsewhere.

"Tell me about Jake," I say. It is not a question.

"Jake?" Rachel two says his name as though she's forgotten who he is.

"Yes," I say. "Jake, my brother. You never talk about him. We never talk about him, do we?"

"What do you want to know?" Rachel two says, and the scissors slow down, and suddenly she's cutting away at time.

"Jake was a special boy, Rachel. Really special." She describes him, but only from the outside. She does not mention his inside. "He was beautiful. You've seen pictures. Those green eyes, always squinting. That fair hair that flopped over one side of his forehead. Everyone loved Jake. He was funny. Always telling jokes. Like your dad. And he was so clever. I will never forget the summer when we went to the Cape. You were just three, Rachel. He built the most beautiful birdhouse you've ever seen. He constructed it from mud, and leaves, sticks, and small pieces of sea glass. The birds flocked to that house." Rachel two pauses, then continues. "Jake loved to run," she says. "I loved to watch him run. I liked the look on his face. I really think he was in another world."

We are interrupted by the sound of the doorbell. It's B.B. Moser. She's dropped by with a present for Grandma's birthday.

"It's a book," she says. She winks, and I hope that it's one of those trashy novels that Grandma likes to read. Instead, B.B. says it's a biography, and I know it's the story of some person Grandma could care less about.

"Thanks, Betty," says Mom. "That's sweet of you." Then B.B. asks to borrow some gardening shears, and Jake is forgotten by everyone but me.

Fisher and I had planned to drive to the shore this weekend and take a run on the beach. But Fish had to spend the day in his dad's law offices doing menial legal tasks. His father wants him to be a lawyer, but Fisher wants to do something else. He wants to be a cook or a glass blower. He says it suits his fragility. Then he asked me how he could love and hate his father so much at the same time. He asked if I thought it was normal. I told him I didn't know what normal was, but that I understood the love/hate thing because it's the same for me. Then we took a late-night run up to the mill and talked some more. There were no surprises. Just the familiar beat of Fish's heart, the falling of night, my own breath.

I think of what Grandma will get for her birthday. Everything that everyone else would like her to have and nothing she really wants. Dad will give her a kit so that she can measure her blood pressure by herself. Mom will get her a scarf that she'll put in her dresser alongside all the others she has been given. Her friends will give her jam and books, a romance or two if she is lucky and they are honest. But she won't get what she really wants. Not unless I give it to her. "Is it so much to ask?" I say to myself. I think of Jake and the car. I have never really purposefully gone against my parents' wishes. But the time will come. The time comes for everyone. Maybe the time for me has come now.

FOURTEEN

I gather together the money I've saved, and walk into town to the pet store. The bakery windows shine with bread sculptures and deep brown loaves, all different shapes and sizes. Long, thin, round, oval, braided. A dozen types of flour stare back at me alongside bread pans, flouring boards, measuring spoons and cups. I stop in front of the pet shop. In the window is a kitten. It is the color of ginger. It's batting a stuffed mouse around its glass cage. I tap on the window and it looks at me. I go into the store. Its gaze follows me and it forgets the mouse.

"She's a beauty," says the woman at the counter.

I ask if I can hold her. The woman lifts her up and hands her to me. The kitten stretches her paws toward me. I feel her little heart beat against my palm and then she starts to purr. Her fur is long and soft like strands of cotton. I cannot let her go.

"I'll take her," I say to the lady. She is going on about vaccinations, fleas, diet, but I am not listening. I cannot take my eyes off the little ball of life that I'm holding in my hand. I buy a carrier, a litter box and litter, some food, and a basket. It takes two trips to bring it all home. Then I buy a nice yellow collar for the kitten to wear around her neck.

I have broken the rules. I have gone against my mother's wishes and gotten a cat. Suddenly I dread going home. I am not afraid of being punished, but I do not want to be judged.

I don't know how I will "let the cat out of the bag," so to speak. There is no one home when I arrive with the kitten. I am struck by the silence of the house, an accomplice to my crime.

"Here we are, kitty," I say. I set her down on the kitchen floor. She scratches to get out of the carrier. I don't have the heart to keep her in. I unlatch the door and she steps out cautiously and wanders around the room, sniffing at the cupboards and in all the corners. Rachel one is the first to arrive. By now the kitten is meowing and purring like an engine.

"Happy birthday, Grandma," I say.

"It's a cat," says Grandma, unbelieving.

"And it's yours," I say.

Grandma scoops up the kitten and sits it in her lap. She starts stroking it. They are made for each other.

"What are you going to name her?" I ask.

"I'm going to call her Pumpkin, after that recipe of yours," says Grandma.

I look at her. Each movement tells a story of what she's given up. Grandpa is gone. Jake is gone. Youth is gone. But she has accepted her losses gracefully. Is this what happens with old age? Will Mom and Dad become like that? Will I?

I bake Grandma her favorite cake, white, with flecks of citrus peel. The lemon explodes in its center like sunshine on a foggy day. The kitchen smells warm and sweet. Grandma and Pumpkin watch me. And I feel happiness swirling around me.

Rachel two comes home. She sets down her briefcase on a chair. "Where'd the cat come from?" she asks.

"I got it for Grandma," I say. I hope if I own up, there will be some room for plea bargaining.

"Here, Pumpkin," says Grandma. Grandma strokes the kitten.

"Where on earth did you find her?" Rachel two asks.

"At the pet shop," I say.

Dad walks in. The first question he asks is, "Has she been vaccinated?"

"Yes," I say, fumbling in my mind for the information that the pet store owner has given me.

I am racked with guilt. I wear it like a ribbon curled around my body.

I cannot bear to look at Rachel two. She does not scold about the cat. Instead she asks if I've taken a shower. I am still in my sweats from volleyball practice.

Grandma gets up and takes Pumpkin out to the garden. Pumpkin starts pawing at Mom's petunias.

"Don't worry," I say. "I got the cat for Grandma. I'll help look after it."

Rachel two doesn't comment. But she is sentencing me. I feel it. Maybe I am sentencing myself, too. Months, years. How many infractions will I get?

We sit down to dinner. Rachel two has made lasagna and Caesar salad. We eat and then we sing "Happy Birthday." Grandma blows out the candles and we have cake.

"This cake is delicious, Rachel," says Mom. Pumpkin is weaving in and out around her ankles. She tries not to cringe. The guilt bubbles and brews, and I try to push it out of my mind. Grandma opens her other presents.

After dinner Rachel two goes out into the garden. She is happy to leave the cat. I watch her from the window with her precious plants and flowers. As always, she changes, opening up like one of those blossoms.

I don't know how she can leave this house. Leave the garden. It cannot come with us. Year after year flowers and trees have come and gone, but they have left their mark on life, buried and turned under the soil. I watch her bend and sway like one of them, and I am happy she has this place to go to.

Today after track practice I worked in the garden with Mom. She had to bribe me to get me there. The daffodils we planted have all burst through like sunshine gathered in a bundle. Mom tried to convince me I have a green thumb, but I don't. I did a little weeding. Then I bent down and turned the soil so Mom could plant some seedlings. She asked me how things were and I said, "Fine." I don't know why I do that. I'm like Hamlet on the stage saying what I think everyone else wants to hear. I am saying what I want to hear. But as time goes on, I see (or feel) that I am forever distancing myself from my family, from myself. Mom and Rachel are planting a beanstalk. They grew it in a jar from a seed and are now putting it in the ground. Rachel wants to know if it will grow up to the sky and lead to a pot of gold. I don't have the heart to tell her that it won't.

I think of the beanstalk. At first it didn't grow at all. Then it sprouted and it grew and grew until I thought it would reach the sky. In my dreams I think it did. But it finally pulled itself in and dried and settled for another year.

Grandma's voice comes to me from across the room where she is stacking plates and putting them away. I am brought back to the present.

"Let me tell you a secret, Rachel," she says. Grandma has a drawer of secrets. "Someday you will know them all," she says. She runs her hand through her lovely white hair.

"Your mother was not always like she is now," she says. "You have forgotten how full of life she was. I often search for the little girl I knew, the woman I knew, but she is a stranger to me now. I remember her laughing at her garden parties. Her pretty round dimples, which have become creases in her cheeks. She is like an injured butterfly who has folded its wings, moving quietly and cautiously through life." Grandma sighs, then goes on. "Mothers and sons," she says. "Jake was her son. I know how it was with your Uncle Edward. It's not the same as a daughter. A daughter is wonderful. But a son for a mother is everything. You know how you used to curl up in your father's lap? How you tell jokes together? Girls have their daddies. Mothers have their sons. Your mother changed after Jake died. She had to, or she could not have carried on. It was too painful. It takes a long time to get used to pain. To live with it like a dear friend. She could not do it. Forgive her, Rachel."

I feel the tears come to my eyes. Then I begin to laugh. Grandma comes to me and hugs me. I want to cry, but I just laugh. When I finally stop, I go out to the garden.

"I'm sorry about the cat," I say.

"It's okay," says Rachel two.

"I should have asked," I say.

"It would have been better," she says. She is pruning the rose bushes. "Want to give me a hand?" she asks.

"You know I'm no good at gardening," I say.

"It's easy," she says. "Like this." She pulls back the branches and begins snipping. She doesn't wear gloves. She says she needs to feel what she's doing. Suddenly she stops to push my hair back and tuck it behind my ear. Just like she used to do when I was small. She doesn't scold or say anything, though I know she hates my hair falling in my face. "How is the house hunting going?" I ask. Rachel two shrugs.

"How will you ever leave this garden?" I ask.

"I can start another one," she says. "Isn't that what life is all about? Starting over."

It is my turn to shrug. I'm the one who cannot leave the house. I'm the one who is not willing to start over.

I brush my teeth and put on my pajamas. Another birthday come and gone. My own birthday is coming up in just two months. My eyes are drawn to my elbow, where I have a birthmark. It is shaped like a horse's head. Adrian used to call it Mr. Ed. Mr. Ed is a friend. He reminds me of who I am. He stretches when I move. In the summer I slather him with suntan lotion. "Good night, Mr. Ed," I say. Then I add, "Good night, Adrian, wherever you are."

Today I had my birthmark removed. It was in the small of my back. A brown coffee stain shaped like a moon. A shadow on my skin. The rest of me is pale and clear. That one reminder that I was born and that I am not perfect. Mom took me to Dr. Moser to have it checked. He is a dermatologist. He scowled and said he didn't like the look of it. Then he said it ought to be removed. He was afraid it would grow and I would become a giant birthmark. A giant reminder that I am. I was afraid of having it taken off. I wanted to wait until after the state meets, but Dr. Moser insisted and Mom couldn't say no.

I tried to be brave. But I was trembling and my skin was crawling in the small of my back. Dr. Moser was dressed in his white gown. The room smelled of alcohol and antiseptic, like my father does. The odor of the operating room has seeped into his skin, and he wears it like an after-shave. Dr. Moser was gentle. He explained everything that he would be doing. I hate needles, but he said I was tough and it wouldn't hurt. Instead it hurt like crazy. I had to hold back the tears. Finally my skin went numb and I had no feeling. Then Dr. Moser cut and slowly and deliberately erased part of who I am. He put a nice clean white dressing on my wound. And he sent my birthmark off to the lab with a date and a label. Mom took me home. She stopped at my favorite ice cream shop and bought me a sundae. While I was eating, the feeling started to come back in my spine. It hurt like hell. It was as though all of my nerve endings were exposed. It was so intense and I felt there was no escape. I guess there is no escape from the pain of being. I kept thinking, *if only I could have cried, the pain would have drowned itself in my tears and disappeared.* But I couldn't cry. I just couldn't.

I don't want Mom to change the dressing. Or Dad. I don't want them to touch my skin. To feel my fragility. So I let Fisher do it. He is gentle and it's okay. He knows how I feel. I can't run for a week. I have four stitches, and it is too painful. The energy builds and I feel that I will explode like a firecracker. I stand in front of the mirror and try to pull myself together. To construct me. For some brief seconds I am all together and I look at myself. Then I just seem to self-destruct into a million pieces that float off aimlessly into the universe.

FIFTEEN

Today is the bread festival. Mom and Grandma were up at dawn baking. I tried to make a lemon loaf, but the dough didn't rise, and I left it sitting there in the bowl like a lead weight. Fisher made wild berry bread. It looked beautiful, light and airy, with bright flecks of many-colored seeds. His cheeks were glowing and he was happy. I was, too. Then along came his father, Fisher Cox the Second. He punched Fisher in the shoulder and called him his Pillsbury Doughboy. Then he started to laugh and Fisher's face fell. His smile turned into a frown, and not even I could pull the corners back up.

The bread festival has arrived. I am up early making my pumpkin loaf. Dad has gone into the office and Mom is out getting groceries. I shuffle through the cupboards gathering together the ingredients I need and reveling in the smell of spice and plenty. I think of Adrian. Last year he was here with his peanut butter loaf. I can still taste it and feel its gooey, gritty texture on my tongue. I brew the yeast. Then I carefully level the flour, just as Grandma taught me. I mix the dough, gather it on a board, and begin kneading. Then I roll it into a ball and wait for it to rise. Mom drops off the groceries and goes into the garden to water the flowers. I poke down the dough and wait for it to rise again. Around noon Grandma comes over with Pumpkin, who sits in the middle of the kitchen, sniffing inquisitively. Grandma has made a beautiful yellow loaf of poppy seed bread. She and I play cards as my bread is baking, and I feel that the warmth of the kitchen, my nearness to Grandma, the cat—all these things bake into my loaf. When I take it out, I am satisfied. It's a lovely deep auburn color and smells of fall. I place it on a rack to cool.

It is late afternoon when we all head into town, Grandma and I with our loaves of bread. The streets are closed off to traffic and lined with stalls featuring free drinks and coffee and games. Rachel one and I leave our entries at the contest booth and take a number. I am glad to be rid of my loaf. I have stuffed myself so full trying to get the flavor just right that I actually think I never want to see another loaf of bread again.

We meet up with the Mosers. Paul and Dad go off to play archery. I'm left with Priscilla. She's baked a blueberry-apricot loaf. Bowman joins us later looking like he's just rolled out of bed. His grapefruit peel loaf hasn't risen and weighs a ton. Bowman, Priscilla, and I walk past the stands. We snack on sausages and french fries. At dusk they announce the prizes. I am embarrassed and turn the color of peaches when they announce the winners. I have been awarded first prize, a cookbook and a small bronze medallion. My name will go down in the annals of the village. Bowman is the first to congratulate me. Soon I am surrounded by family and friends. I am drowning in praise and happiness. I would like to seal this moment in a vacuum jar to keep forever, but I know it can't be done.

That night we gather at the Mosers'. Paul prepares a barbecue of roast chicken and peppers. The talk revolves around Bowman. They are all speculating on his future. Or perhaps I should say deciding whether he should take a year off or go straight to college. Everyone has a different opinion. Bowman is angry. It is the first time ever I've heard him raise his voice. He scolds us for not living in the present and says there should be no past or future. I glimpse an inside of him smoldering like the matches he is forever lighting. I am dismayed, as is everyone else. Something sinks in and we are silent. Dad changes the subject. At midnight B.B. brings on the lemonade and everyone toasts me and my pumpkin loaf. But we are all still thinking about Bowman.

Fisher's berry bread won second place. It felt great until Fisher Cox the Second showed up. He shook his son's hand and slapped him on the back. Then he joked that Fisher might not want to put this honor on his résumé. Fisher did not laugh. He came home with me and sat in Claire in the driveway for over an hour. He cursed his dad and swore he'd be a garbage collector before ever becoming a lawyer. Then he sat back and closed his eyes and wondered aloud what it might be like if I just floored the motor and we sailed off over the cliff into nothingness. He sounded serious and I dared to think what it might be like to float above the earth, Fisher's and my spirits linked forever. And I liked the idea.

Cars.
Big metal chunks lined up at the curb
painted pretty like a rainbow.

Round and round the wheels go in never-ending spirals.
Bright smooth shiny headlights push into the night.
Fast cars, wheee

Uh oh, car breaks down, out of gas,
and the driver frowns.

SIXTEEN

When I go down to breakfast this morning the newspaper is spread across the table like a precious drape. There I am on the front page of Grandpa's paper. I have set a state record for the 100-meter dash and the hurdles. The camera has caught me just as I am about to leap. I look sure and fine. The headline reads: "Soaring into the Unknown." Underneath is an article. It states that I have broken three previous records this year. I am the son of a doctor and a judge. I am a brilliant student. On it goes, singing my praises. But as I read about myself I do not know this person who is being described. The black-and-white of the picture has hidden the insecurity, the doubt, my crawling skin. I do not recognize those legs sailing across the hurdles.

There is no mention of that strange discomfort I feel so often. The camera has not caught that. It has only captured the top layer of a life.

The next morning my name is in the newspaper announcing the winners of the bread contest. But it is not as it should be. The names of the winners are usually on the first page. This time they have been pushed out by a more dramatic event. The old mill by the river has caught fire in the night. It has nearly burned to the ground. The firefighters are still working to squelch the flames and contain the damage. The lines of newspaper blur into one another as I read. There is no explanation of what caused the fire, but the possibility of arson is mentioned.

As I read and reread, I feel the searing heat of the flames against my own skin. I feel my own history meld with a bigger history that encompasses more than I can imagine. I think of my grandfather and his drive to spread the news, good and bad. And I think of that stupid joke: "What is black and white and red all over?" Suddenly I start to giggle. Rachel two comes into the kitchen. There is a softness I rarely hear in her voice.

"I played up at the mill as a child," she says. "On the big wide lawn under the apple trees."

I must leave for school. I collect my books and start down the road, one turn after another heading toward town. I must pass the mill to get there. I don't want to see its frail skeleton heaped on the ground. I don't want to concede the truth of all I have just read. I want to roll myself into a ball and shoot down an endless gutter that takes me back in time. The smell of fresh-baked bread has been smothered by the acrid odor of burning embers. And the flour mist that filled the air yesterday has turned to smoke. I force myself to look. The fire-fighters are still hard at work. What's left of the mill is surrounded by a crowd of curious spectators.

I think of Bowman and I remember his childhood wish. To be a fireman. Then I recall what he has said about the past. I remember his matches, what he has said about fire. His anger. I feel the cold just as he's described it nestling in the layers of my skin. I remember his words, and I want to forget.

At school everyone is talking about the fire. Like all tragedies it has a grotesque appeal.

"It's a crime," says the English teacher. I think of Rachel two.

"Is it a crime?" others are asking. All are speculating. I do not utter a word.

After school I find Dad home from work early. He is closeted in the study with Paul Moser, and they are speaking in hushed voices.

Rachel two is in court today handing out sentences

for other crimes, or absolving those she believes to be innocent. I go into the garden. I am alone with myself and my thoughts. Thoughts I do not want to have but over which I have no control. I have never before minded being by myself. Now I do. I reach out and touch the petals of a flower. Every now and then a bird screeches. I am surrounded by life, but right now I feel terribly alone.

Today I was at Fisher's house when his dad cornered him and asked if he'd received his replies from his college applications. "No," said Fisher. Then he announced that he'd be deferring any acceptances. When his father asked him what he thought he might be doing in the meantime, Fisher said he was thinking of taking cooking lessons or maybe a course in glass blowing. "More like blowing your future!" his dad thundered. He shoved Fisher into the wall and slapped him across the back. "Over my dead body," he shouted. Then he kicked Fisher like a poor stray dog and sent him on his way. Fisher's father was so angry that tears were running down his face. And for a moment it looked as though he was crying. Maybe he was. Why does it matter to him so much?

Fisher was in a daze for the rest of the day. I took him for a ride in Claire, and he broke down and told me that his father had been like that his whole life. A tyrant to Fisher and his mother. I thought of my own father, who has never laid a hand on me. Whom I have never seen cry. And I thought of the bond that must bind Fisher to his father to have made him cry. And I thought how screwed up it all was. How screwed up we all are.

I asked Fisher how his mother could stand it. He said she bore it because she believes in reincarnation. In another life. She believes our spirits will return in some other place and form. She has not put all of her faith in this life. Like so many of us have. Like maybe I have.

Once there were two boys. Jake and Fisher. They dreamed of running away. Of cutting themselves off from the invisible threads binding them to this earth and the people in it. They dreamed of being free. Free to laugh, free to cry, free to live, and free to die.

I am lying in the dark drifting in and out of sleep. Scenes from my own life pass back and forth before my eyes. Downstairs Mom and Dad are laughing about something. They are good and decent people. I have not been abused, as Fisher has. I do not have that excuse. I do not want to make them cry. I don't want to be blamed for that.

The weekend is finally here. I have not slept well for days. Rachel one comes over. I haven't seen her since the bread festival, since the mill burned down.

She kisses my forehead. "I am proud of you," she says. Then she goes on. "Good news, bad news. Isn't that what Grandpa always said. Life, just like newspapers, is composed of columns of each. It's a shame about the mill," she says. But she is placid, accepting. She takes out her knitting and begins to work.

"Can you show me how to knit?" I ask her. I am looking for a distraction.

"Knitting is for old people," she says.

"Come on, Grandma," I say. "That's not true."

"Sit down," she says. "Get some yarn and needles. Over there." She points to a cupboard filled with unfinished pieces Rachel two has begun. I choose a ball of thick red wool.

Grandma wraps her hands around mine and walks them through the movements. "What are you going to make?" she asks. She hums to help me with the rhythm.

"A scarf," I say. I want to knit a scarf for Bowman. For next year, when he goes off to college or wherever he goes. I want a scarf that he can wrap around himself like a cocoon. A red scarf that will keep him warm so that he won't need his matches. So he will forget about fire.

I work slowly. Then I pick up speed. A calmness spills over me. And as I watch the red square lengthen, I realize I am knitting into my scarf all of my feelings, anger, sadness, and happiness.

Mom is knitting a sweater for Rachel. She asked me to hold the yarn while she turned it into a ball. The pretty green woolen lengths of fluff disappeared and a big green ball grew in its place. She had the patience to knit row after row each evening. I made fun of her and said it would be easier just to buy a sweater. And she said it wouldn't have her hands and their strokes in it. She is right. I know what she means. I always liked holding those hands walking to school. I still can feel how it hurt to let go. Then I dreamt that I woke up with her hand in mine but it was detached from her body. And I freaked.

Now Mom has put away her knitting. She is cutting out paper dolls for Rachel. Her clever hands curve and circle and carve away at the paper and, voilà! I couldn't do that. I'm not good with my hands like she is. I couldn't be a surgeon like Dad, either. I don't have that sure grip and those solid fingers. My hands are long and my fingers are so thin and wiry that they tangle like weeds. Fisher took my hand the other day and opened

*my palm. He began to trace my Life Line. And the
lines for heart and head. His mother says our hands are
a secret map of our destinies. Each infant holds his future in its small fists. I wonder if this is true. I stare at
my hands for what seems like hours. At the different
lines, routes, some of which finish in dead ends. And I
do not know which way to go.*

I don't know how much time elapses before I put down
my knitting. My fingers are tired. My hands are
cramped. I make a fist and stretch my arms full length.
Then I lay my hands in my lap, palms upward. I look at
the blue veins etched like roadways leading up to my
wrists. The fine lines carved into the skin. Life, heart,
head. I trace them back and forth with my finger. Then
I close my fists gently, hanging on tightly to the precious life I have.

EIGHTEEN

I feel like I am shrinking, like Alice in Wonderland.
Like I have eaten a mushroom and I am finally growing smaller. I cannot stop the feeling, the sensation that
in this universe I am forever tinier and more insignificant. I have not seen Bowman for days. He hasn't
called. He's not at school. I continue to knit the scarf
faster and faster as though I am racing against time.
Sadness sweeps over me again and again. I think of
Adrian. I do not want him to slip away. The more I
knit, the faster my hands move, the more slowly the
scarf seems to grow. My arms are sore and tired, but I
cannot stop. Then at some point my fingers become
numb. I become numb. The bell rings. It's Betty Moser
at the door. Dad greets her, leads her into his study, and

closes the door. I can't stop the doubts that are growing inside of me. I want to cry but I cannot stop giggling.

Rachel one is in the kitchen preparing dinner. She has brought Pumpkin with her in the carrier.

"I didn't have the heart to leave her home alone," she says. She is apologetic, and I know she is thinking of Rachel two.

Pumpkin comes into the living room and pounces on the ball of red yarn. She begins batting it around with her paws. At last I put the scarf down.

"They say cats have nine lives," I say to Pumpkin. "Why can't people have nine lives?" I want to know.

Today I took a pair of boots to the cobbler for new heels. I commented to Harold, the cobbler, that it must be nice to be able to fix things, to make things new again. I jokingly asked him if he could fix me. "What's wrong with you?" he wanted to know. "You look great," he said. I told him I needed a new soul with an extra tough backing. Unbreakable and waterproof, if possible. At first he laughed. Then he looked me straight in the eyes and he stopped laughing. I was afraid he would see what I was all about, so I turned and ran. And I didn't stop until I'd reached home.

Run, run, as fast as you can you can't catch me I'm the gingerbread man. I feel like the gingerbread man. They have mixed the ingredients, rolled the dough, cut me out, given me eyes and buttons. But I must go and they must let me. Will I be eaten by the fox?

NINETEEN

I have hurt myself. I pulled a hamstring playing volley-ball. The pain is unbearable. A burning sensation spreads through my thigh. Dad picks me up from practice. He ices the muscle. He says I must stay still. I have no choice because it hurts even to breathe. At home I settle on the couch and I pick up my knitting and continue with my scarf. I begin to get used to the pain. Then it spreads eerily through my body until it's as if the muscle bears the pain of all of my losses.

I finish Bowman's scarf. And I fold it and put it in my drawer. Grandma offers to lend me some of her books. Then she begins rattling off advice she's stored up from her years of writing columns. How to remove water stains from wood surfaces. How to mend a torn sheet.

Her tangents are like live visits to the past. Then she is back again, lucid as ever.

"How do you mend a broken heart, Grandma?" I ask. "Didn't you tell me that once?"

"Has your heart been broken?" she wants to know. She comes over to me and runs her hands through my hair. Then she kisses me on the head.

"Sort of," I say. "Or it's about to be."

"The trick is to breathe. To move with the pain," she says. "All of the body regenerates, heart included and spirit, too. Otherwise we couldn't go on, Rachel. We break legs and arms. They mend. Hearts and spirits mend, too. That's the miracle of life."

She says these words, but I am not sure she really believes them. I am not sure I do. Pumpkin winds around her legs, and Grandma reaches down and picks her up.

"I am glad you got me this cat," she says. "So glad."

Dad comes to me. He moves my leg in small circles. Then, as he wraps a bandage tightly around my thigh, he tells me what I have known all along. That it was Bowman who set fire to the mill. He has been charged with arson. There will be a hearing, but I already know the outcome. I know it is true. I witnessed the matches, the cigarettes, Bowman's fascination with fire.

"Even when Bowman was a little boy, he was always

wanting to play with matches," says Dad. He is sitting on the edge of the sofa, but he is off in the past somewhere, delving for bits and pieces that will make sense of what has happened. Then he starts rambling, like Grandma does.

"If we could only see more clearly, then maybe we could stop some things from happening. We all have eyes, but our field of vision is so small." I know he is not just talking about Bowman. He is voicing his despair as a human being. As a doctor. As a father. There are many forms of blindness that cannot be cured.

Bowman will graduate from high school at the top of his class in two weeks' time. And less than a week after, he will be tried for arson. I burst out laughing as though it's the funniest thing I've heard in ages. But I feel an open sore festering in the pit of my stomach. Dad sits there helplessly fidgeting with his pant legs. "Life is not easy, Rachel," he says.

"Why do you think Bowman did it?" I ask.

"I don't know, Rachel," Dad says. He throws his hands in the air and goes on. "I suppose it was just a way of acting out his feelings. Anger. Confusion." He goes on. "I guess we expect a lot from our children. Especially boys. Sometimes in our attempt to keep them safe, we lead them into a den of lions. I am as guilty as anyone else," he says. I know he is thinking about Jake.

I see the muscles of his jaw tense. "The body, the mind are so complicated."

It's the first time I've ever heard him admit this. Admit defeat. Admit that we are only human. I must remind myself that he is a doctor and he bears the weight of our failings. In the end we are just people with faults and flaws.

"The truth is parents make mistakes, Rachel," Dad says.

"People make mistakes," I say.

Dad sits there for a long time with me. A silence descends. It is one of the good silences that nudge us painlessly, reminding us that we are alive. Dad's presence makes me feel good. He looks out the window into the garden. The iris is in full bloom. I know he is with Jake. We both are.

I am sitting in a silence with Fisher. We are waiting for the school day to finish. The world is spinning around us, muffling its sounds with its own movements. I am thinking of all of the different kinds of silences there are. Peaceful sleepy silences like a field of poppies under the noonday sun. Silences charged with the power of a tidal wave. And there are dead silences. They are the worst kind, when the world feels like it might come to an end.

Dad and I do not hear Mom come in. Before we know it, she is standing before us, reminding us that for Bowman this is a first offense.

"I hope they'll go lightly," she says. "The trouble is the mill is a historic monument. It's not as if he's burned down any old building."

"What will happen to him?" I ask.

"Bowman's not yet eighteen," she says. "He is still a minor. I expect he'll have to enroll in a treatment program. He'll need counseling." Now she turns to Dad.

"Arson is an illness," he says. Suddenly they are both in their uniforms. "Something's gone wrong in the mind," continues Dad. "Arson is an obsessive type of impulse."

"Bowman is a good person," I say.

"Sometimes good people do bad things," says Dad. But I am no longer listening. I am thinking about Jake.

I am standing in front of the mirror looking at myself naked. I do not really know what I am looking for. Maybe a clue to who I really am. I flex my muscles and hold. It is tiring to hold this stance of strength and force. My eyes wander over the smooth skin, the bulging muscles. Then I relax and give in to the truth. Without my track uniform, without my clothes, without my muscles, I feel lost.

I have never seen my parents naked. Are they anything like me, I wonder? Fragile and soft. Is there something of sameness besides the skin and bones? I dress myself and feel the layers of clothing burying a truth that is only visible when I am naked.

Dad keeps on talking. But I don't want explanations. Scientific or moral. I am trying to get them to take their uniforms off. But they won't. It occurs to me that I, like Jake, have never seen my parents naked. I have never seen them vulnerable. I have never seen their birth-marks or their scars. They have always been clothed in the guises of order, justice, healing.

Twenty

Bowman's name is in the next day's newspaper. Just as mine was a week ago. It's there on the front page with a black-and-white photo, in the paper that Grandpa founded fifty years ago. Miraculously, the press has cured his acne. His skin is smooth and clear. I read how he is described: "a tall and lanky teenager who loves books." Then, a few lines later: "an apparently troubled adolescent with a fascination for fire." An account of the fire follows and finishes with the usual question. Why? There is a string of possible explanations. Frustration, depression, anger, rebellion. Are his parents to blame? Is society to blame? I wonder again, does there always have to be someone or something to blame?

The article begins on page one and then continues

on page twelve. It faces the sports page, which features the results of the weekend's state track meet. The photos and names of the winners decorate the page—smiling, clean-cut adolescent boys, just like Bowman. Just like Jake. I begin to doubt those smiles and what is behind them.

I tear the article from the newspaper, fold it, and put it in my drawer, along with my other keepsakes.

By the following day Bowman has drifted into anonymity. He is forgotten as the senior graduating students gather in town in the square in front of the library. They are dressed in white and they're carrying buckets filled with flour. Some of them have smeared paste across their cheeks and bodies. It is like a riot as they run through the streets tossing fistfuls of flour to the wind. The shop owners have come out to watch. The police are there, too, to keep law and order. The rest of us observe from the sidelines. School is in session, but no one is studying. No one is really there. We are all in the street, reliving the past that flows through us, that lives in the air we breathe.

I walk home from school past cars dredged in flour. Flour lies like patches of snow on the asphalt. It hangs weightlessly in the air. I inhale puffs of it and I cough. It settles in my hair and on my clothes. There is no getting away from it. The students are breaking up now. I watch them disperse. And I see Bowman. He is covered from head to toe in white. But I know it's him. I know by the way he moves. I know by the short shirtsleeves. He is swinging an empty bucket. He sees me. He knows I am watching. But he does not wave or speak. He simply disappears into the crowd.

I go home and I shower. I rinse the flour from my skin and hair. The water runs over my body in thick streams, and I realize that the past is no longer huddling on the doorstep, as I imagined. It's in here with us. It's been here all along. Sleeping in our beds. Crouching in our closets.

As I stand under the jets of water, I relive the past few weeks. I relive Adrian's departure. I relive the moments spent with Bowman. And I relive Jake's death. I relive it a hundred times.

TWENTY-ONE

Today my acceptance to Princeton came in the mail. They are so happy. I have made them ecstatic. What an incredible power trip. My father is drooling. My mother glowing like a neon light. I could make them so sad, too. But do I have the courage to wipe up that spit and flick off that light?

After dinner I go over to Fisher's.

"Golly, by golly," croons Attorney Cox. Fisher's dad stands there stiff as a board in a shirt and tie. Then he holds out his hand and shakes mine like a man for the first time ever. He slaps me on the shoulder in the same way he is always slapping Fisher, and it hurts. Then he actually pours me a drink. This is the same man who snarled when he caught Fisher and me with a beer.

"What'll it be? Whiskey or gin?" he says. So my acceptance to Princeton is an I.D. as well.

"Orange juice," I say. But he pours me a drink anyway. A gin and tonic. Then he pulls out an envelope and waves it through the air. He clears his voice, stilling the world, and the clock nearly stops. In the envelope is Fisher's acceptance to Yale. I don't even know if Fish has seen it. Anyway, there we are standing before Fisher's mom and dad like two brightly polished stones. Fisher's dad seems to have forgotten his conversation with Fisher about deferment. Fisher is unusually quiet. He seems to have forgotten, too.

What a sight. Mr. Cox glowing like embers in the grate. The DNA popping. It's too much for me.

"Wheee," I holler and I run around the armchair. I jump over the coffee table. This would not have been allowed before my getting into Princeton. But now it's okay. Anything's okay. "Whooo," I shout, and Mr. Cox slaps me on the back again and everyone has another drink.

I go home. Reality settles in. I open my palm and begin to trace the lines carved in its creases. Why am I not happy about getting into Princeton? Hundreds of guys would kill for this. I know what it means. I've started down a road from which there is no turning back. I don't feel ready. I don't have the tools. If I go to Princeton, I will keep on running. I will never be able to stop. I watch the sun setting and suddenly I feel alone. I am afraid of the feelings that steal in and sneak up on me, winding their way around me like an agile rope. I inhale them. Fear. I sure know that one. It makes me catch my breath. I don't want to be alone. Or in the dark where anything can happen. I go to bed, but when it grows dark I get up and put on a light. I see everything that is there before me. But the trouble is it is still dark inside of me. I have no internal light and I will never be sure what is there.

I have piles of French homework that I have left undone. I could not be bothered putting it on paper. Still, I cannot stop conjugating verbs in my head. Etre is the verb to be. Je suis. I am. "To be or not to be," said Hamlet. I am. But what am I? That is the question.

Fisher picks me up and we take a run around the lake. We lie in the tall sweet grass side by side. Fish is sweating. The air is heavy. Suddenly I feel I can't breathe. Fisher is telling me that he's changed his mind. He is going to Yale after all. In a new red car that his parents have promised him. He says it is impossible to say no when his name is already engraved on a plaque outside his father's office. Then he says, "I am an only son.

You know what that means." It means he is going to study law like his father. I am pissed. What has Fisher's mystical mother done? Hypnotized Fisher in his sleep, cast a spell over him? Well, I guess so, and the magic has gone deep. I do not have the antidote. I am not able to reverse the spell. He is going. Fisher is going. I get up and run across the grass, through the woods. The branches pull at me. Fisher follows me. He is calling to me. But I will not stop. I run until I can run no more. Then I collapse in a field. A bug who lacks the decency to not crawl over me tickles my skin. It's a reminder that I am alive. But I do not want to know.

Fisher has betrayed me. He's off to Yale. He will have a brand-new car to take him there. A little sports car with his initials on the plate. He is following in his father's footsteps and not mine, like he promised. There will be no reincarnation for Attorney Cox. It won't be necessary. He will just live on in Fisher's body. And Fisher will die. Someday he will remember that he, too, did not like cars as a little boy. And someday he will be sorry.

TWENTY-TWO

Once there was a boy named Jake . . .

When life becomes nothing but one big feeling, it is time to bow out.

I have found what is left of the Matchbox cars I had as a child. I saved a few for Rachel, who liked to play with them. They are small, innocent toys.

Tomorrow all the graduates will flour themselves and gather in the streets. But I won't be there. As darkness falls, I will take the sacks of flour that I have brought to the garage where that beauty of a new sports car waits for me. Car. A small word. One of the first words we learn. I'll wet her down with a damp sponge. At first I'll toss small fistfuls of flour onto the hood. Then they will become large handfuls. Then sacks. I'll cover the car until it looks like a ghost. After, I will cover myself. Then I will climb into the driver's seat and back out of the garage. Who the hell am I? The son of a doctor, the resident of a certain street. Where the hell am I going? I am fuckin' lost. I will reach into the glove compartment for a map, for the shortest route to paradise. I have an appointment with God. Here I go. I feel the car moving, faster, faster. I feel energy charging through the universe. I am soaring high, dancing with the angels. Their sweet and heavenly smiles are holding me up. And their robes are fluttering around me. Their golden halos frame my head. Wheee! Whoooaa! That's all, folks!

At the back of Jake's journal there is a newspaper clipping with a picture of Jake and the article about his death. It appears in the newspaper that my grandfather founded. The same one that had my prize in it. The same with the photo of Bowman. You cannot run away from the past. Or the present. Or the future. I am sorry. Sorry for Bowman. Sorry for Jake. Sorry for my parents. And sorry for myself.

I am holding this newspaper when I go downstairs. I am wearing Adrian's sweatshirt. Rachel two is telling Dad about another house she's seen and loves.

"Want to come see it, Rachel?" she asks. "I think you'd love it." I shake my head.

"I won't love it," I say. I begin to talk and cannot stop. "I went to Jake's room," I say. "I found Jake's journal. I read it." Rachel two is not wearing her robes, but in my mind I see them draped over her shoulders and I wait to be judged.

"We've never forbidden you to go to Jake's room, Rachel," she says.

"You never talk about Jake," I say. "You never talk about that room." I am accusing her for her years of silence.

"Jake is dead," says Rachel two. But she is lying. He is dead, but not for her.

This bigger truth starts smoldering in the air. And so many other truths float to the surface.

"Jake floured his car and drove over a cliff," I say.

There is a silence. Not a dead silence. It is full, ripe, and weighty.

The silence is broken. "I know," says Dad. "Jake took his own life." He can barely say it. He feels it like I do. The years have not tempered the blow. Rachel two pours herself a glass of water, but she does not drink.

Suddenly the anger melts. A sadness floats down from the heavens and envelops us all.

"You know what I really want?" says Rachel two. "I don't really want a new house. I want what I can't have. I want Jake." She breaks. And she is naked there before me, all of the scars showing. Deep and painful.

I am not forgiving. "Why have you never talked about Jake? Why didn't you tell me?" I ask.

"So often, Rachel, I don't tell me about Jake," says Rachel two. "He seemed so perfect on the outside, but inside it was a different story. Jake was a troubled boy. He was lost. We tried, Rachel, but we could not help him find his way.

"The room," Rachel two goes on. "That was my way of coping. Of not letting go. I used to go in that room and I could still smell him. I could still feel him. But it is less and less as time goes by. I don't want to lose that. That scares me, Rachel. I couldn't bear going into that room and not being able to smell him or see him there before me. I thought maybe moving would help."

I am holding tightly on to Adrian's sweatshirt, afraid that it may dissolve in my hands, before my very eyes.

Dad speaks again and I see why he does not want to look in the mirror. Why he does not want his picture taken. He doesn't want to be reminded of the pain that he carries around locked in the folds of his skin. In his gait. In the tilt of his head.

"All parents lose their children, Rachel. They grow up and grow away," he says. "We will lose you, too. In a manner of speaking." Now his voice is hoarse. "We lost Jake early on. We weren't ready. We couldn't understand it. We still can't. Something went wrong. I couldn't fix it. Your mother couldn't fix it. Maybe our not speaking was a way of protecting you, Rachel. It was not a way of protecting us. When you are hurt that deeply, it does not matter what other people think. You become immune to that. It was to protect you, Rachel." He stops. Then he goes on. "Many years ago, Rachel, it was a sin to kill oneself. For many people it still is. We didn't want Jake to be remembered like that. We didn't want you to know him like that."

I look at them and I realize how hard it was for Jake, how hard it is for all children to expose their cracks and breaks to their parents, especially if they have never shown us theirs.

"Happiness eluded Jake," says Rachel two. "He was in paradise when he was running. But you can't run through life. We could do things for Jake, but we couldn't breathe for him. He had to breathe for himself." Rachel two is bent over with tears in her eyes. She stands before me, and I see a tree blown and battered by the wind, shielding the branches that have been lost until it can sprout new buds.

Suddenly Dad speaks. "Do you think we parents just get angry and holler?" he says. "We cry, we suffer, too. Sometimes we're afraid."

"Jake did not see that, and we didn't help him," says Mom.

"Maybe we all need our gods," says Dad. I remember what Bowman said. Jake was his god. Fisher was Jake's god. I think of my gods. The captain of the volleyball team. Adrian. My own parents.

Suddenly I am in a daydream, that place in between that Jake talked about so often. His angels are there, hanging threadlike in midair. They are singing softly. I am waking up from one of life's long sleeps. The wind blows open the window and then the door moves back and forth and the curtains billow. The dust rises from the floor and is swept up in its currents.

I realize that this is not just about Jake. It's about Adrian. And Bowman. They, too, have left me.

"It is hard to be hurt by the people you love," says Dad. "It is hard to hurt the people you love. But it happens. We are only human. We have defects."

All the truths rain down upon me. Why I always choose boys for friends. Why I don't want to be friends with Priscilla. It is not because she wears heels and nail polish. It is because I am looking for Jake. In my mind I am journeying silently. And only sometimes do my movements betray me. I am following the dead. I am resurrecting him in all my friends. My mother has done the same. My father, too. Each time he saves a life. Each time a patient dies, he hopes for a glimpse of the afterworld, hopes to see Jake one more time. Each time my mother serves justice, she is seeking to be rewarded, seeking to right a crime that has no right. The cold truth dawns. Jake is gone. He is not coming back. He is never coming back. I cannot free myself of him, nor can they. Nor can Fisher, wherever he is. The tears come to my eyes. They are like small wells overflowing onto my cheeks. I wait for the laughter. But this time it doesn't come. The tears do not stop, and I worry that maybe they never will. I want to laugh but I cannot. I can only cry. I cry for days. For Jake. For Adrian. For Bowman. For my parents. For myself.

Today I laughed so hard I cried. Laughing and crying are all the same. An explosion of emotion from within. Did you ever see the clowns at a circus? Aren't they laughing and crying at the same time?

TWENTY-THREE

Jake has written about forgiveness, in the margins of a page. It is the last thing he writes.

Forgiveness comes after a long time. After a long and gentle rain of tears. The earth is soaked and the smell of springtime is in the air. New life will come. Look for me in the flowers and the trees. When they wave in the breeze, think of me moving, running gracefully. And please please forgive me. I have forgiven Fish. I have forgiven myself. I have forgiven that guy on the corner who spit on my foot so many months ago. I have forgiven today, which could not help but come. I have forgiven yesterday, which could not help but pass. I will forgive tomorrow, too.

Forgiveness is hard. It's the truest thing Jake ever wrote. I have not forgiven Adrian for leaving me. I have not forgiven Bowman for his crime. I have not forgiven my parents.

Forgiving means letting go. And I don't want to let go of any of them.

Jake is buried not far from home. Not far from Grandma's. In the plot beside Grandpa and a lot of other relatives I know only by name and birth date. I've been there each Memorial Day. I go again. And I think of what he wrote about forgiveness. He does not have an epitaph. It is simply his name and date, and I remember how he would like to be remembered. I will remember him as a sweet breath of life passing through.

I walk home through town, past a block of office buildings. Polished bronze nameplates flank their entranceways. I stop and watch the people coming and going through the revolving doors. I think of Fisher Cox. In my head I build a composite of how he must look. At the same time I am reminded of Bowman's people-watching and his observation that we are all disconnected. We are all standing on the same earth, breathing the same air, journeying through life alongside family and friends. But at the same time we each have our own separate journeys that have to be taken alone, our own private struggles and griefs that cannot begin to touch others.

At last I get the courage to take the scarf I knitted for Bowman out of the drawer. I wrap it in colored paper. After dinner I walk the many blocks to the Mosers'. B.B. answers the door.

"Is Bowman at home?" I ask.

"Hi, Rachel," she says. She cannot hide her surprise. Her worry about what I know of Bowman. About what I think of Bowman.

"Bowman," she calls. "Rachel's here." Bowman comes tripping down the stairs in a shirt with its usual too-short sleeves. He doesn't look any different. I am glad to see him.

"Hi," I say.

"What's up?" he says.

I feel very tall and awkward. "I just wanted to drop this by," I say. "It's something I made for you to take with you in the fall. To school or wherever you're going."

"The reformatory?" he jokes. And he laughs. I see the other side of the pimpled face. How hard it must be to live with those pits and scars. To laugh at them when you want to cry. I remember him laughing at them.

"I am really sorry, Bowman, that this had to happen to you. I told you you shouldn't play with matches."

"I know, Rachel," he says. "I just couldn't help myself. I don't know why I did it. It was dumb."

"We all do dumb things," I say. "Some dumber than others," I can't help but add. We look at each other for a very long time.

"I'm sorry, Rachel," he says. "I'm sorry I did that."

"Don't make me cry," I say.

"You'll just laugh anyway," he says.

"No, I'll cry," I say. "And I might never stop until I drown us both."

Bowman takes the package and unwraps it. He winds the scarf around his neck and grins. It looks nice on him. That is what I remember. That is what I take with me. The image of Bowman with his scarf and a smile. The smell of coffee coming from the kitchen. The sound of B.B. Moser on the phone.

TWENTY-FOUR

When I get home, I find Mom standing in the middle of Jake's room. She has begun to box up Jake's things. I look at the cartons. FRAGILE—HANDLE WITH CARE is stamped on their sides. I think of Jake's T-shirt. He did not realize that we are all fragile in our own ways. That we all need to be handled with care.

"Are you really going to be able to leave this room?" I ask.

"I don't know," she answers. "I often find myself hoping that when we pack the boxes and empty everything, we will float skyward. We will be free. Part of me wants that freedom. But another part of me does not want to let go."

Moving does not seem such a terrible idea. This

house has conspired to keep Jake hidden. It's an accomplice in crime, to use my mother's words. But, I, too, wonder if the secrets, the misunderstandings will disintegrate, or if they will be packed up and moved into a new house.

Today in class we talked about freedom. Freedom to choose. To vote. I kept laughing inside. All of these freedoms only to be bound by self. I will never be free from myself. Free of my mind. Only in death and maybe not then. I cannot free myself from the urge to run, to shout, to cry, to be. Sometimes this is the most terrible bondage of all.

Mom leaves me in Jake's room. I sit down on the bed like I did not so very long ago and look around at the objects. Each speaks to me. Each says something about Jake. I hear Grandma downstairs, cleaning up the dinner dishes. Pumpkin is meowing loudly.

"Shoo," says Rachel two. She will never love cats. *Superstition is nothing but fear.*

"Come here, Pumpkin," I hear Grandma cooing. "Mind your own business."

Dad is working late. But he'll be home soon. He will make some joke about his day. This is his way of coping. And it's not a bad way. Maybe I will become a comedian after all, now that I can laugh without crying. I stand up and do a little monologue for Jake. About this girl who laughed when she was supposed to be crying. Then I sit down on the bed and I enter the past. The past *can* be entered. I know that now. It's dusk, and darkness is falling fast, as it does in late spring. I go to my room. I have never said a prayer for the dead. But now I do. I bless the living and I bless the dead. And I hope that in this life or that in some way or another they have all found peace. I take a book from my shelf, a collection of stories. Jake wanted a story. I open the book and I start back down the hallway. I begin to read aloud. The sound of my voice echoes off the walls. But as I read, another voice comes to me dreamlike from another place and time. It is my mother.

"Walk softly, Rachel," she is saying. "You'll wake up Jake." But now I know that I won't wake up Jake. He has gone forever. Into a deep and peaceful sleep.

"Goodbye, Jake," I say. "Goodbye."